DEATH BEYOND THE NILE

Also by Jessica Mann:

A Kind of Healthy Grave
Grave Goods
No Man's Island
The Sting of Death
Funeral Sites
Captive Audience
The Sticking Place
Troublecross
Mrs. Knox's Profession
A Charitable End

DEATH BEYOND THE NILE

Jessica Mann

St. Martin's Press
New York

fiction
(mystery-suspense)

 For information, address St. Martin's Press, 175 Fifth Avenue, New York, N.Y. 10010.

Library of Congress Cataloging-in-Publication Data

Mann, Jessica.
Death beyond the Nile.
I. Title.
PR6063.A374D4 1989 823'.914 88-30174
ISBN 0-312-02564-5

First published in Great Britain by Macmillan London Limited.

First U.S. Edition

10 9 8 7 6 5 4 3 2 1

Prologue

When the sun disappeared with an abruptness to which the Europeans could not get accustomed, darkness fell immediately and the air became very cold. On the rocky shore a row of little fires flickered. Beside each of them two or three Nubians crouched by the warmth as they prepared their evening food. The diesel generator on the Europeans' barge began its laboured chugging and the lights flickered on. Very briefly the pestering wind slackened, and the sounds of flapping ropes and tarpaulins, of water against the metal sides of the barge, of whistling air through awkward crannies, mercifully ceased. The cacophony would return with the dawn.

Nobody had expected the noise. Everyone except Tamara Hoyland had expected to be laid low by what the others called Tutankhamun's revenge. She, who believed that you were only ill if you allowed yourself to be, crouched suffering in an unlovely lavatory cubicle.

In the saloon on the covered deck her companions were assembled, she supposed, to give the imported whisky and the local wine their nightly chance to loosen tongues. There was to have been fresh fish for dinner. One of the Nubians had brought his catch for them to admire before delivering it to the galley, a basket full of strange pewter-coloured creatures with predatory teeth.

Tamara shuddered at the thought. Discomfort and intermittent waves of real pain rippled through her intestines. She hoped that she would be able to leave this, one of only two water closets on board, before an impatient queue built up outside it.

Footsteps were coming downstairs. Was dinner finished already? But the feet trod gently past the locked door, and along the passage off which all the cabins led. She could not tell which one they entered but it could only have been to fetch something for in a little while they came back and went upstairs again.

Cloacina, prayed Tamara, little goddess of the sewers and of those who use them, what name did the Egyptians give you? For surely in the country for which the expression 'gyppy tummy' had been invented, some deity received the prayers of all who suffered it. Roman goddess, local version, guardian angel, you must have made your point by now. My pride went before this fall, Tamara had to admit to herself, wondering whether to say to Miss Benson that she would use some of her much vaunted homeopathic cure-alls, or whether she could bring herself to beg one of Vanessa Papillon's miracles of modern pharmacology.

Other footsteps. It sounded like old Solomon, slightly shuffling. He went straight past into his cabin.

The spasms did seem to be passing. Tamara waited a moment, braced against the craft's swaying on the water. She decided that the worst was over and opened the door into the dim corridor.

A third person had been down, someone whose footsteps she had not heard, for a flash of green fabric disappeared from view up the stairs. None of the servants wore green, a colour reserved by Moslems for those who had made the pilgrimage to Mecca and avoided, perhaps from tact, by the local Christians.

The boy had already turned the sheets down and brought back the washed and pressed laundry. A night shirt was folded on Tamara's bed and she put it on before lying down.

But she was thirsty and the bottle of mineral water was empty. With a peevish sigh she got up and padded barefoot to the pile of crates under the stairs. At least she could not blame her indisposition on the water supply, for like everyone else in her party she was careful to drink and clean her teeth in the water that had been sealed into its plastic bottles somewhere in Greece. Only Giles Needham and his staff arrogantly dared to swallow what the lake provided and even to swim in its waters.

Tamara turned back towards her room. It was at that moment that she heard the scream, a rough, harsh, awkward sound that seemed infinitely shocking.

It was Timothy Knipe. He was standing in the open doorway of Vanessa Papillon's cabin. She was lying dead on her bed.

1

'So there I was,' Tamara Hoyland said. 'About as far as one could be on this earth from help or authority, stuck in the middle of nowhere with a dead TV star, an hysterical poet, a catatonic novelist – not to mention my charges; the one I'd come with and the one I left with.'

'And convinced that it was murder,' her employer said. She wondered whether he felt remorseful at having sent her into that fray, but dismissed the notion.

Mr Black was not one for regrets. A man who was could never perform his secret role, that of running a branch of the government service known as Department E, so secret as not even to have a secret name. Even Tamara herself, who had worked for Department E for several years, could hardly define its duties; and would not try. Her relationship was with Tom Black alone. She satisfied herself that what he asked her to do was what she thought should be done, and what, in various esoteric lessons, she had learnt to do. Further recognition or justification had never seemed necessary.

Mr Black had asked Tamara to go to Egypt with Camisis Tours. The assignment had not turned out as he expected – but the unexpected was exactly what Department E existed to control; and its agents were men and women of curious skills and unpredictable intuitions.

For some time Tamara Hoyland had simultaneously been employed by Department E, and been a member of the staff of the Royal Commission on Historical Monuments from which she had resigned just before Christmas. That had been her first job after finishing her doctorate at Cambridge, and she had been in it for seven years; long enough to know that she could stay there for the rest of her career, gradually ascending the promotion ladder; making a contribution in her chosen speciality; respectable, respected, increasingly expert at recognising and describing the material remains of the past. It was what she had wanted to do and she had enjoyed doing it, but enough was enough. Moonlighting had spoilt her for real life.

It was after her lover, Ian Barnes, had been killed in the service of his secret department that Tamara had been recruited to work for it. She had never intended to do so for long. Her self-image was not that of a spy, nor was she sure that she entirely approved of the aims, still less of the methods, of her second, unadmitted employers. She was ashamed to recognise that she loved the work. But she was hooked on the excitement that went with it. Using the dangerous skills that she had acquired was thrilling.

And of course, Department E, unlike other more open branches of the civil service of which it was part, paid its employees extraordinarily well. That had come as a surprise to Tamara. She had not considered the financial aspect of the work at all, and queried the unexpected addition to her bank account after her first assignment. She earned a retainer, and large sums after active work.

To keep on working at the Royal Commission in a job that was worth doing for its own sake, simply for the valuable cover it provided for secret activities, was too cynical for Tamara. In any case, in telling everyone that she was leaving to get on with her own work, she was truthful. Her former professor, Thea Crawford, had repeatedly told her to publish in academic journals. Mr Black, that reserved, disguised man, saw another side to Tamara's nature. His suggestion that she might turn to writing fiction was infuriating. Tamara had hardly admitted even to herself that it was something she would like to do. This was by no means the first proof of his omniscience. All his young people had to resign themselves to the fact that Mr Black knew everything that research could uncover about them. But Tamara had never mentioned this slightly embarrassing and completely private ambition to him or anyone else. He had said:

'You know as well as anyone that insight is what our profession requires. We construct convincing models from incomplete evidence just as you do when you jump from a few potsherds to a whole theory of prehistoric economy. We think, but we also feel – the attributes of a creator.' Tom Black himself was the author of pessimistic, anonymous verses.

'I am not sure that I have the imagination required,' Tamara said.

'Call it clear-sighted intuition, then,' the poet said to the archaeologist and added, as spy master to agent, 'I require you to speculate and to observe.'

But for spies as for archaeologists speculation can only be useful when based on information. Discreet researchers had been detailed to produce dossiers on her travelling companions, while Tamara Hoyland, thanking her stars that she was a quick study, taught herself something of the Egyptian past in the intervals of sorting out her thin clothes and taking a rapid course of inoculations – and of pitying the professor, who had undergone the same discomfort only to withdraw on mendacious pretexts from the journey after patriotic persuasion, so that Department E's emissary could take his place.

The Egyptology was easier to understand than the contemporary problems that were on Tamara's hidden agenda. It was an aspect of archaeology that had never especially appealed to her. Magnificent though its remains were, they were the result of millennia of absolute control by an invincible governmental organisation. It was remarkable that such autocrats and bureaucrats should have held sway in a period when the people on whose material remains Tamara usually concentrated were illiterate peasants; but not attractive. Nor, being as it were tone-deaf to religious speculation, was Tamara inspired by the idea of a people for whom the whole of life had been a preparation for death. All the same, even someone lacking what a modern atheist once called 'a God-shaped hole in his consciousness' could not fail to be excited by the chance to see the stupendous remains of that priest-ridden civilisation.

'You were right about one thing at least,' Tamara told Mr Black. 'By the time we were near the southern end of our voyage, I found ideas jumping about in my head. Ideas that I'd suppressed for years. It must have been the result of reclining on the deck, floating past real life that never touched us. We were in a kind of capsule, protected, out – literally – out of this world.'

'And then your great novel turned into a crime story,' Tom Black said. 'One of your characters had committed a murder.'

'Every single one had the means and the opportunity,' she said. 'The whole lot of them could have done it.'

'You were sure it was poison?'

'That much, yes. But what poison, or where it had come from . . . It was like a nightmare. And as for opportunity, we all had it. It made me wonder which of them had come there specifically to get an opportunity. Was it mere chance that gathered these particular people in that particular place at that particular time?'

'Your mind turned to the occult?' he said sceptically.

'It would certainly have fitted into any fictional version. Not to mention the sex, snobbery and violence; the murder, mystery and romance, with a touch of the supernatural, and The Curse of the Mummy.'

But Tamara knew that it was not, in fact, the beckoning finger of a mummified ghost that had drawn these people together. It was the appeal of Giles Needham himself. His series of programmes had appeared on British television during an especially nasty patch of winter weather. The tropical landscapes before which he appeared were attraction enough without the need to postulate supernatural influences on those who vowed to be somewhere sunny this time next year. All the travel companies that offered warm winter holidays increased their profits that season.

It seemed perfectly reasonable to assume that the party on the Camisis tour had been collected together by no more irresistible force than chance. At the time they made their bookings, 'Egypt was in the air'.

Giles Needham was not the only leader of this fashion. Even before he joined other scholars unexpectedly bounced into notoriety by a television appearance, fashion magazines had been sending undernourished girls to pose in foolish garments on camels beside pyramids; boutiques were selling clothes on which the mask of Tutankhamun stared, distorted by the curved flesh beneath; and the best-selling board game of the season had been based on hieroglyphics.

Not even his most envious colleagues could have accused Giles Needham of jumping on a bandwagon. He had already directed three seasons of excavation at Qasr Samaan and had published numerous articles about Egyptology. It was pure fluke that the place of work where he was filmed with his classic profile silhouetted against a vermilion sunset should have seemed like paradise to so many people.

'I was pretty keen on the idea myself,' Tamara recalled. She had not been immune to the charm that enthralled so many gawpers on successive winter Wednesdays.

'I', said Tom Black, 'would have been pretty keen to

go on any excursion accompanied by Max Solomon.'

Tamara said, 'I can't help feeling that reading his journal is . . . I don't know what. A privilege. A sacrilege.'

'Fortunately,' Mr Black said, 'I have no such inhibitions. I found it a fascinating document. It only seems a pity that it broke off so abruptly. You could have used this man's perceptions.'

'But he stopped perceiving anything after Vanessa died. He turned entirely in upon himself.'

'Up to that point, he was a camera.'

'As, until then, he had been for the whole of his life.'

2

From Max Solomon's Diary: February 1.

Osmond of Camisis Tours greets the members of my party as they arrive at Heathrow. They are wary and peer at other travellers' luggage labels to see what company they have let themselves in for during the next three weeks. I am apprehensive too. A courier's journey can be hell or heaven depending on his charges' attributes.

I lurk in the bookstall. Like everyone else in the departure lounge, I see Vanessa Papillon. She sweeps by with an undirected smile. She is not only recognisable, but in some way more alive than anyone else. In her wake other women take out their compacts or glance at themselves in reflective surfaces.

I read the front pages of all the daily papers. They blazon the disappearance of Princess Mary. A small paragraph in *Private Eye* last week hinted at the girl's absence without leave from her college. It seems that the fact, if not the imputed motive, is true. Princess Mary has been kidnapped from the holiday cottage of the girl friend with whom she was staying.

The girl is not important in politics or ceremony. She is a long way from the throne. But she has attracted attention all her life. Now her abduction has become an affair of state. Her personality and appearance are discussed as though she were a film starlet. Old tales are repeated and new ones are invented (or so I suppose) of her wilfulness, arrogance and determination to get her own way. I think the implication is that she has brought her fate upon herself.

Osmond of Camisis joins me in my discreet corner. With him is our lecturer. It is not Professor Thomas. A family emergency has forced him to back out at the last minute. Dr Hoyland has stepped into the breach, Osmond says. She is small and brightly coloured, I think by nature not art. She must be older than she looks. She treats me respectfully, but we rapidly form the usual alliance against the rest of the group. It is the paid against the paying passengers, us against them.

I ask if all of them have turned up. Osmond has ticked everyone off. 'Dr Macmillan is in the loo,' Tamara Hoyland says. 'I read the name on her luggage label.'

Osmond goes off to charm the others. Tamara Hoyland and I lurk behind the racks of paperbacks. From the front page of each newspaper the same face stares up: Princess Mary. The most recent picture was taken at an undergraduate dance. She has untidy hair half across her face and her eyes are screwed up against the flashlight. Her dress is slipping from her large breasts and she holds it up with one hand.

Where is she now?

What would I do if it were my Jonty?

I turn the page of the paper I have bought, and expose a photograph of starving children in the Sudan. Brutalised by habit, I am less affected by it.

I do not introduce myself to my party until we are in the aeroplane and have had lunch. I do not eat much. I cannot dispel a certain horror at the Daedalian hubris of modern travel.

They have chosen seats in widely separated rows of our aeroplane. Dr Macmillan, who is on her own, is at the back, where she chain-smokes. Vanessa Papillon and her companion, who is, it seems, a poet and has greeted me as a colleague, have paid a supplement to travel first class. Mr and Miss Benson, with Mr Bloom, have won the row of seats by the emergency exit, and sit in greater comfort than I do.

I observe the new lecturer. She has a sheaf of papers on which I recognise the Camisis monogram. I have seen the instructions that Osmond gives his scholars. He advises on clothes (casual) and medicines (numerous) as well as the standard of the lectures (popular) and the nature of the response to queries from the paying passengers, which must be polite at all times and in all circumstances. The duration of each talk is specified. Five minutes at Esna, ten at Edfu.

'I wasn't reading about the trip,' Tamara said.

Mr Black paused almost reluctantly, his slightly mottled, liver-spotted hand gentling the pages of the notebook. With uncharacteristic absent-mindedness, he said, 'Weren't you?'

'I was cursing your stooges for leaving it till the last minute to provide me with some dossiers. The messenger met me at the very doors of the departure lounge.'

'But the material was useful?'

'I think it had been compiled by another of your novelists manqué. And later on, of course, I could add to it myself.'

The system, designed to meet an emergency, was makeshift, but the people who operated it were benevolent and it worked as well as could be expected. All the same, the label tied to the coat of the child who would later be known as Max Solomon had disappeared. Perhaps he had picked it off himself. There was nobody who seemed able to identify him. He seemed to be between three and five and he was mute. He stood in the reception centre staring around him with large grey eyes under straight, strong brows, and gave no sign of understanding anything that was said to him. Nobody could discover his name, or where he had come from or even in what language to address him. His composure was infinitely touching.

At the end of the day Bertha Solomon could not bear to let the child go to the hostel. She took him to her own home in Muswell Hill where her husband, a busy, preoccupied surgeon, accorded him the gentleness due to a stray kitten.

The child did not react to what he saw, neither to the comfortable furniture nor the lavish food, to the black skull-cap that Jonathan Solomon wore for dinner or to the seven-branched candlestick on the table. He sat where he was put, and swallowed what was spooned into his mouth. He allowed himself to be washed, he used the lavatory, he slept silently on the bed in Jonathan Solomon's dressing room.

The Solomons decided to keep the child. They called him Max after Jonathan's father, and said that it was a temporary solution since his own family would reclaim him sooner or later. They enjoyed having him so much that they hoped, guiltily, that it would indeed be later. But very soon it was clear that it might be never, for the long-expected war broke out and the fate of Max's blood relations was only too easily imagined.

By the time the war ended Max was effectively an English boy. There was no telling whether the tongue that spoke the language so fluently had ever used another one. As far as Max was concerned Bertha and Jonathan Solomon were his mother and father, and he admitted to no other memories. Sometimes Bertha would think she could trace a faintly Slavic cast to his cheekbones or a southern fullness in his lips. Outsiders simply saw a handsome, healthy lad, not even noticeably Jewish except in the eyes of those who knew he must be. Nobody would have guessed that he had once been a small speck of flotsam from the European hurricane.

In later years Max's wife, Ruth Solomon, would say that they were foolish to worry so much about giving their son Jonty a happy childhood, when Max himself seemed so unaffected by early insecurity. He had satisfied the ambitions of the most optimistic parents with scholarships at school, Oxford and Harvard; with a prize for his first novel, a film made of his second, and his name on students' reading lists by the time he had written five. A generous and perceptive critic, a fluent and amusing broadcaster, a successful author of elegantly sardonic fiction, happily married, as English as they come – Max Solomon had it made.

Max never realised how dependent he was on Ruth. He would have said, if asked, that he could manage on his own, that he was self-sufficient. He would have said that he and Ruth were a partnership of equals, together from choice not need, that Ruth gave him a hand to hold, not a crutch to lean on. He was more surprised than anyone else at the loss of his powers after she died.

Ruth had always said that his ideas bubbled up from an everlasting spring. 'He's an ideas man, he never runs out,' she told the interviewer from the *New Yorker*, whose three-part article was entitled 'The Ideas Man'.

Now there was a drought. The well was dry, blocked by the dead body at the bottom of it.

'My invention was cremated with my wife,' Max Solomon told his publisher. He had not written a word of fiction for three years.

'But you can still write something,' Jonty Solomon said. The inventive impulse would return, he insisted, when Max least expected it. Meanwhile he could exercise the writing muscles with description and analysis. 'Write journalism, like me.'

But Jonty could not imagine his father's loss of charity. Observation must be softened with it, if the reporting is not to singe the paper. Max had no charity left, except for Jonty himself. Everything else he saw through the ice of his frozen sensibilities.

It was Jonty's friend, the psychotherapist, who sent Max Solomon on his travels. She was wrong in promising that it would do what she called unblocking, for after seven journeys Max was still not writing a novel, but the strange places distracted him, and when he was far from home he did not always have Ruth somewhere in the periphery of his vision. In Bombay or Buenos Aires he did not imagine that the back of every dark head or every high, half-heard laugh was hers.

The therapist said that Max was living too much within himself. What he had lost and needed to retrieve was the outsider's eye, that external vision that had often seemed a burden in the past, so much so that Max had once consulted another psychiatrist about the *doppelgänger* that he felt watching his every action. He said then that he wished to live unselfconsciously. But now, objectivity lost, he realised that it had been the foundation of his power to invent.

At least when he was abroad he could watch new sights and see strange people. One day he might again find that he was watching himself.

Even writers as successful as Max Solomon are unlikely to amass enough money for the silent years. He took a post as courier for Camisis Tours, conducting parties to China, Kashmir, Mexico, India, Argentina and the South Seas. He was a draw.

But Egypt? Max was not sure that he wanted to go there again. He had seen it with Ruth.

Once a week Jonty Solomon took his father to lunch. This time they had met in one of the expensive, short-lived restaurants that cluster around Covent Garden. The food looked prettier than it tasted. Jonty pushed heart-shaped slivers of salad and liver around a heart-shaped plate. Max's raw fish was masked by a blue sauce representing the sea.

'Bilberries, perhaps,' he suggested. It was not entirely appetising.

'You ought to go to Egypt, Father. Especially on this trip, right down into the south. There might not be another chance to get into the lake like that.'

'The Nile cruise must be beautiful. Did you see that programme?'

'*Death on the Nile*?'

'I meant the one with that archaeologist. Giles Needham's piece about Qasr Samaan, where the Camisis tour is going.'

'My boss fell for him in a big way.' Jonty worked on Vanessa Papillon's programme. Once, when she was ill, he had presented it.

'Has he been on *Butterfly Net*?'

'Not so far. He actually said no. It's unheard of. Vanessa was furious. She's in hot pursuit. She always wins.'

'How?' Max asked.

'She's going to be on the Camisis trip. If you go as courier she'll be in your care. I suppose I shouldn't wish her onto you,' Jonty said.

'She travels alone, does she?'

'Not this time. Her last bloke walked out on her and she's got a poet at present. You know the kind of chap, cashes in on looking like an Elizabethan pirate, and preys on women as though he were one. He is said to have left half a dozen kids and a wretched wife somewhere in East Anglia, and some other bereft female in Cambridge,' Jonty said.

'I should like to see you doing Vanessa's job,' Max said.

'My dear Father. Not a hope. You know her; that voice, those looks – how can I compete?'

Vanessa Papillon's famous voice was inimitable, literally; many mimics had tried. It was a contralto with a resonant undertone like a plucked cello string. She had amber eyes and streaked tabby hair that defied gravity to stick out like a cloud around her head. Once a politician had stroked it unthinkingly; and failed to get the incident edited out of the programme, although he protested all the way to the Chairman of the Board.

Max Solomon could not deny Vanessa's beauty and fame. But he believed that his son's talent was equal to anyone's.

'You stood in for her once. Everyone said you were marvellous.'

'And I have never been forgiven.'

'You'd be better than she is. You should have your chance.'

'Over Vanessa's dead body,' Jonty said. He looked out of the window.

Jonty was bored by talk of the woman with whom he spent so much of his working life. He said, 'I wish I could understand why snow seems so nasty here when one pays so much to see it in a ski resort.'

'Osmond of Camisis says that in southern Egypt it never even rains.'

3

Dr Hoyland sees me watching her. She says, 'Mr Solomon, I might as well admit to you that I'm a fraud. I am not really an Egyptologist at all.'

My heart sinks. It is I who will receive the complaints if the lectures are not good enough. I say, 'You mean you aren't an archaeologist?'

'No, that's what I am. But I haven't specialised in the Middle East. I just hope that nobody will notice.'

'If that's all . . .' I say, relieved.

'Mr Osmond was desperate for a replacement lecturer at short notice.'

There has been a good deal of short notice about this trip. Three people dropped out, an elderly widow (to my relief) and a couple of Americans. Dr Macmillan made a very late booking, the Bensons and Mr Bloom later still. There were vacancies on the package because of its expense. My company comes expensive.

Osmond was not specific about what stopped Professor Thomas from coming. An ill-omened expedition?

The separate members of the party do not meet until we are all standing at the customs tables in Cairo airport, where Mr Knipe first catches sight of Dr Macmillan.

He calls her name so loudly that even the vendors beyond the barrier cease their shouts for a moment. 'What the hell are you doing here?'

'I am on holiday.'

'Here? With Camisis?'

'I have been wanting to visit Egypt for ages,' she says. She stares at him with what looks to me like a kind of defiance. She looks tired, more so than a four-hour daytime flight can explain. She has orange hair and a pale, drawn face, and fixes pale eyes on Knipe. He shouts:

'You bloody liar. You had never even heard of the place before I . . .'

Miss Papillon's voice professionally tops his. 'Won't you introduce me to your friend?' But she is interrupted by the customs officer, who wishes to search her cases. He must be one of the fundamentalists who disapprove of provocative women. We pretend not to watch him feeling through the lace underwear and chiffon nightgowns. He pokes suspiciously at films, cassettes and tampons. Then he empties out bottles of tablets, and demands that she identify each.

She goes through them, as we all pretend not to listen. Her pharmacopoeia includes an alphabet of vitamins, something to stop the squitters, as she puts it, something to avert malaria, to prevent sunburn, to induce sleep and to ensure wakefulness.

'So many drugs,' Miss Benson says. She has already told several of us about her devotion to homeopathic remedies, many of which she has brought with her.

'Drugs?' The customs official knows the word, only too well.

'No it isn't drugs,' Miss Papillon snaps. 'Do I look like a hophead?' It is obvious that the man knows quite well that these are permitted medicaments and is enjoying himself.

I begin to feel that it is unlikely that I shall do so during the next two weeks.

'I certainly doubted whether Janet Macmillan would enjoy herself in the next two weeks,' Tamara said. 'Me, you had sent on a wonderful free holiday, at least that was what it felt like so far.'

'Not a fool's errand, then?' Mr Black asked.

'Oh, don't get me wrong. I thought it was. After all, I had just been reading what your researcher thought about Janet Macmillan. I think he missed his vocation as a gossip columnist.'

'You ought to know where the best information comes from,' he said.

'Charwomen? Party tattlers?' Tamara's nose wrinkled as her courtier ancestress's must have done at the reminder of things that were beneath her. 'All the same,' she admitted, 'it was quite useful at the time.'

A typical product of that close-knit kinship system of the academic upper classes, Janet Macmillan was the daughter of a dead economist and of the first woman to have become Principal of a Cambridge college that had formerly been for men only. Janet had climbed straight up the conventional education ladder, had the usual number of previous affairs and experiences, and was knocked out by love, of a kind, for Timothy Knipe. She said he was the first man to teach her that there was a difference between the head and the heart.

Timothy had not been invited to dinner with Janet's Managing Director in his Old Rectory just outside Cambridge. Timothy was to stay in the flat watching – and remembering to tape – Giles Needham's last programme.

Janet's social evening had industrial implications. She worked on the development of medical machinery. Her own special interest was in electro-encephalography. The guest of honour was Russell Kopelovitz, an American scientist working in the same field. He was tipped to win a Nobel prize.

Hugo Bloom was there. He was one of those successful businessmen drafted in to give the benefit of their entrepreneurial skills to an ailing Health Service and in a position to steer valuable contracts towards the firm. There was a professor of surgery with a dim wife and a professor of psychology with a drunken one.

The Managing Director glanced regularly around his table. There were some subjects that he intended to have discussed. His wife had been briefed.

Janet told the surgeon about her new interest in ancient Egypt. She hoped to go there with Tim, who had introduced her to the subject on which he, and therefore she, was passionate. They would see it when they could afford to; but he had five children, and she helped out with their maintenance. Her Managing Director had not invited Janet that evening in order to hear her tell the man from Addenbrooke's about the Pharaohs. He was relieved when he saw his American visitor turn from his hostess to Janet.

Hugo Bloom, on the other side of the narrow table, was the target of heavy flirting from the drinker who, having discovered that he was not married, began to make impertinent guesses about his private life. She had elicited that he had come over from Fernley where he spent most weekends.

'I know all about it,' she said loudly. 'Arty farty sub-Bloomsbury with madrigals.'

'I play the clarinet,' he said.

'I'll bet it costs you. I saw their brochure. Lots of stuff about their priceless ambience, with a hefty price tag. Anyway, it's probably poisoning you.'

'We eat very well,' Hugo Bloom said, putting a sliver of duckling into his mouth.

'I'll bet, considering how often I've seen Ann Benson in the cash-and-carry buying your ready-cooked meals for the deep freeze. But I didn't mean that. Don't you know there's a government research station next door? I'd be worried about radiation sickness.' The woman's chatter masked the fact that Janet was telling Kopelovitz a little too precisely about results that might have a commercial application.

Janet was at her best, her employer thought, enjoying the glitter of her tight rings of red hair, and freckle-sanded skin. She was prettified by love, even if it was for a useless layabout who claimed to be a poet. It was not surprising that she held the attention of Professor Kopelovitz; or that Hugo Bloom clearly found her far more attractive than the lush on his left.

A good time in Janet Macmillan's life then; professional recognition, personal happiness. It lasted, perhaps, another three weeks; until Timothy Knipe went on the television chat show called *Butterfly Net*. Janet watched and taped it, and it must say something about her nature that she never wiped it out. It followed immediately on the last of Giles Needham's programmes; the one that had been shown on the evening of the Managing Director's dinner, and taped by Tim for Janet to see when she got home.

'Upped and left, from one day to the next, just like that,' according to the cleaning woman Janet employed two mornings a week. 'Early November, it must have been. I could tell she'd been crying and the dustbin was full of all his gear. He'd walked out on her.'

Had he written? Once, that Mrs Gosling knew of. 'A postcard; he asked her to send all his books about Egypt because he was going there for a holiday, and not to forget the ones about Giles Needham's dig because he was going to go there too. Such a shame, when Janet had been saving all that time to go there herself. But she didn't send the books. I saw them on her desk. The card was in the bin.'

That must have been at the same time that Janet's job blew up in her face too, though neither Mrs Gosling nor, later, the researcher knew anything about that.

Janet had been summoned to a meeting at which the Managing Director sat in like a biased umpire.

The Man from the Ministry, a smug bureaucrat with a closed mind, and Janet Macmillan, began from such different standpoints that it was hard to imagine their parallel minds ever being able to meet.

Even if Janet had been able to produce a logical argument for what to her and her friends and family was an axiom, he would not have been interested. The free dissemination of scientific results, to her almost the entire foundation of her ethical beliefs, was a meaningless concept to him. Personal reticence and public candour was what Janet's code required; his, the opposite.

'Nothing you say could change my masters' minds,' he told her.

'And you can't change mine,' Janet said.

'I, however, have the law on my side.'

'I have never signed the Official Secrets Act.'

'It is the law none the less. It is equally applicable to those who are ignorant of it and to those who have admitted that they understand its provisions.'

'If I accept the risk of being prosecuted you could never stop me publishing,' Janet said.

'I could. Easily.'

'Abroad?'

'Even abroad. Unless you become a traitor. Not a pretty thought.'

Janet said that she would think about it. She was not left in much peace to do so. The Managing Director was as adamant as the civil servant.

'The firm would rather you didn't publish anyway. We ought to get a government contract that will be worth far more than we can make on the open market.'

'But think of the good it could do,' Janet pleaded.

'Think of the harm it could do. You hadn't considered that.'

'I have. And I don't believe it,' Janet said.

'You get the results. It's my job to decide how to apply them.' The Managing Director thought of his clever young research workers as, in a way, his children. It was for him to guard them against a predatory world.

'I don't think I can just leave it like that,' Janet said.

One had occasionally to be firm with children for their own good. He said, 'I must remind you that all lab results belong to the firm. Read your contract.'

'That is fair enough when it is a commercial matter. But this is an advancement of knowledge. It is a scientist's duty— '

'Don't say anything you will regret. Go home and sleep on it.' He patted Janet's head, enjoying the sensation of her springy cushion of hair.

She went, not home, but to a travel agency, where she specified the date and the tour she wanted and did not seem to care that it cost nearly twice as much as any other because so few other people would be on it, and because it would take them where none of the others could. She paid for the trip by credit card and left Cambridge after telling, not asking, her employer, on February 3.

4

February 4.

The faces sort themselves into names and the names into personalities. So far they are relatively untroublesome. Miss Benson has lost her passport twice. Her brother cannot bear people who lose things. These groups always include the same mixture of types. Vanessa Papillon is the prima donna who knows that the other members of the party are gratified to get to know her. There is the passenger who thinks he is slumming – Mr Benson – and those, of whom there are several, who think themselves lucky to be here and (alas) lucky to be here with me. Soon one of them will start the conversation about the underpayment of serious writers.

One of them does.

We also have among us the inevitable know-all. Timothy Knipe, our bearded poet, wishes us to understand how much he could tell us about Egyptology, if he would.

And, as usual, there are the foreign travellers determined to keep in touch with home. They oblige us to hear the BBC news broadcasts. Princess Mary is still missing. A ransom demand has been received. It is in the girl's own handwriting. Three plane-loads of food and medical supplies must be sent to famine victims in the Sudan before the royal hostage is released.

*

We have seen the sights of Cairo and Giza, marvelled at the Pyramids and been disappointed by the Sphinx. We have set sail southwards. At dinner I am at a table with a group who perform the inevitable rite of comparing their medicaments. Two of the party are already laid low with diarrhoea. Everyone has brought an armoury of prophylactics and treatments. The doctor among us, whose wife tells us that he brought a fully stocked medical bag, is one of those already prostrated, conveniently early since he should be well enough by the time others fall ill to treat them.

Numerous postcards have been bought and written. They are put in an open box for posting. The inquisitive flick through to see who has written to whom. 'No secrets among friends,' Lady Gentle says.

Tentative friendships and alliances are being formed. Several of the men are clearly attracted by our lecturer, and no wonder. None dares to be tempted by our butterfly, ditto. Mr Bloom seems to be making up to Dr Macmillan. As they are two of those who have paid for the optional excursion into Lake Nasser to see the excavations at Qasr Samaan, he will have a chance to press his suit. I am glad that Osmond agreed that I could join that trip. Only eight of us are to go. The others will stay in the hotel at Aswan, jollity enforced upon them by our Egyptian guide, as it was by Pai Lee on the Yangtse, Dolores in Peru and holiday-job Penny in Bali.

'The jollity at that stage was more like a London cocktail party than anything enforced by some package-tour cheer leader,' Tamara said. 'Vanessa Papillon was a great one for a kind of flirtatious needling. The domestic version of what she did on her programme, I suppose. Somehow she knew what people were about – I've no idea how she discovered, though she had had more time for her preparatory research of course than I did. And of course it was being perceptive and witty that made her so successful. The unpleasantness was a by-product.'

'You found her unpleasant?'

'Uncomfortable. For example, she had heard of me – not as an archaeologist either. She said that some colleagues had mentioned meeting me on Forway. And she knew about Ian.' The island that had been the home of Tamara's dead lover had been the scene of her first assignment for Department E. Vanessa Papillon should have known of neither. 'And she'd say things about writers and being published, pinpricks of malice, you know? Because it was such a long time since Max Solomon had written anything and of course Timothy Knipe hardly ever got into print at all. It all made for a certain tension on board.'

'Max Solomon doesn't seem to have noticed it,' Mr Black pointed out.

February 5.

We are cruising serenely up the Nile. Everything is going well. We are to leave the ship at dawn tomorrow to see Dendera before the crowds.

Tamara said, 'Max Solomon was so sweet. He wandered round looking benevolent. Everyone said that he made the atmosphere of the journey pleasant. I heard people composing the letters they meant to write in his praise to Camisis. But he was not much better than I was at keeping track of his flock. At Dendera we lost Janet Macmillan.'

The Camisis bus drew up at the entrance of the temple of Dendera before the sun was high or the air was warm, and before there were any other vehicles in the large park. Sayeed, the Egyptian guide, had told Tamara that at Dendera it was for him to explain everything. Union rules forbade foreign lecturers to speak on the site. Tamara took the opportunity to peel off from the group. She found that the custodians had not arrived at the temple. The lights were not turned on. She wandered around in the semi-darkness, going alone into small chambers and up shadowed stairways. Bats flew past her head, and lizards skittered away from her feet. She dimly discerned through small light-shafts, or in the gleam of her torch, carvings and bas reliefs, and silence, emptiness and mystery. It was awesome. She would not have been surprised to hear the voices of the gods themselves rebuking her trespass.

She found a shallow flight of steps, so worn as to have almost become a ramp, that led to the roof, a flat rectangle, bounded by a low parapet on which earlier visitors had carved graffiti long enough ago for them to be not shocking, but poignant, a pathetic bid for immortality. Who had James Mangles and Charles Irby been, visitors of May 1817, who John Gordon or Ignatius Palme? When they saw Dendera its high chambers and columns were muffled by dunes of sand. Now, looking down from this roof one saw, far below, the passengers from the Camisis ship, still obediently concentrating on what Sayeed was telling them; the remains of a Coptic church, the mud brick fortifications, the sacred lake now filled with rustling bosky palm trees – and with a red-haired woman, almost hidden between two flame trees, talking to a robed Arab and at this moment handing something to him.

Tamara ran. She tore across the roof and down those smooth stairs, through the chambers, lit now each with its own bulb, all mystery banished, dodging the attendants, out onto the dusty forecourt and towards the only trees within miles. But Janet Macmillan was no longer among them. A man wearing a brown galabieh and head-dress was crouched there, and rose at Tamara's approach ready to conduct her around. He did not understand, or would not answer, when she asked about the other lady. Walking casually Tamara rejoined the rest of the party. Janet Macmillan was not in it. As far as she could tell, everybody else was.

Tamara edged close to Max Solomon. 'Have you seen Dr Macmillan?'

'Isn't she with us? I believe she came from the boat.'

'I know she did, because she borrowed my sun cream. I really want it now but I can't see her.'

'I wish I could lend you some but I don't use it.'

'I'll go and see whether she left it in the bus.'

A few other buses and cars had parked outside the temple now. Vendors were setting up their stalls of cottons and leather goods. Tamara brushed aside offers of mummy beads, guided tours or small straw dolls.

There was no sign of Janet Macmillan here. Tamara used her smattering of Arabic and the Camisis bus driver's smattering of English to discover that he had seen none of his party since they entered the temple compound. She doubted whether he would recognise any.

What on earth should she do now? She was damned if she would reproach herself. The idea was risible that she could stick like a limpet to any single passenger for the hundreds of miles of cruise, through the numerous sites they went to see, in a strange country where she had no official standing and whose language she hardly spoke.

Tamara had been half-hearted from the outset of this assignment and had accepted it more because she wanted to see Egypt than because she thought it was worth doing. If the authorities were so determined to prevent Janet Macmillan from passing on the details of her invention they should have persuaded her by rational argument. The woman was hardly a fool, after all, and there was no reason to think that she was a traitor. What was more, if she was convinced that the scientific world had the right to know of her discovery, whatever it was, and that humanity would benefit from it, she was as likely to be right as the baboons who, in Tamara's experience, staffed the ministries where such assessments were made.

Tamara was just deciding to quit when she saw a gleam of orange behind the temple parapet. Janet Macmillan's startling hair brought a sense of relief for her watcher, who had almost persuaded herself that she did not give a damn. She pulled her tiny binoculars from the breast pocket of her denim shirt. Yes, it was Janet. She was talking, seriously and apparently not unhappily, to Timothy Knipe. He held out his hand. She shook her head and stepped back, out of sight; it looked as though Tim was about to follow her when Vanessa Papillon appeared beside him. She stood magnificently at the edge of the roof. If the ancients had not placed a woman's statue there, they should have done. Tamara snapped a quick photograph, though she would have had time for others. Vanessa must have known quite well what she would look like standing in that prominent position, and from it must have seen that not only the main group of her own party but many other visitors were by now gazing at her. Happily, she posed.

February 6, Luxor.

Another invariable aspect of these journeys is that one member of the party will lose something and suspect theft. Usually it is an item of electronic hardware. Our doctor, recovered from his stomach upset, is convinced that his medical bag has been interfered with. I offer to inform the tourist police, at which he changes his mind. 'Perhaps I was delirious when I was ill,' he says. 'Or maybe someone was desperate for a sleeping pill. It doesn't matter.' There is a general feeling of unease at the thought of the local police or civic authorities. The passengers tell each other horror stories of people who have been flung into foreign gaols without trial for minimal driving offences or on unfounded suspicion of drug dealing. Nobody wants to get involved with officialdom.

Before dinner Sayeed, our Egyptian guide, delivers a severe lecture about the smuggling of antiquities. It is his patriotic duty to make sure that no part of the local heritage, no matter how insignificant, is removed by a greedy tourist. In any case, he says, anything vendors offer them will be faked.

Vanessa Papillon has done a programme about fakes. She speaks of them knowledgeably, and of the art market. 'Nothing easier than to fake the rather inferior antiques and pictures that sell so well these days,' she says. 'There's money in the Newlyn School, and Victorian genre pictures. Not to mention Egyptian antiquities. Isn't that right, John?'

Not as much money as he would like, Mr Benson says. He quite clearly cannot bear people who claim to know as much as he does about his own subject.

'Oh yes I forgot, you're an art dealer, aren't you?' the poet says, and Mr Benson mutters that he cannot bear people who ask what one does.

Vanessa says that Mr Benson deals in moderately modern pictures and moderately ancient antiques. It is remarkable to me how much she has already found out about us all. Journalistic training, no doubt.

Tamara said, 'The dossier you had organised for me was quite imaginative about the Bensons, and rather inadequate about Hugo Bloom. There was nothing that explained why those two always behaved as though they were doing him a favour by associating with him.'

'You liked him?'

'He was highly intelligent. Very successful – even I had heard of Blooms of Belfast, and you know how ignorant I am about business. He'd been in Egypt before, as a soldier doing his national service, stationed in the canal zone. He said he was so ashamed to remember how he and his mates had treated the natives that he had to make up for it this time. He still had some phrases of Arabic, and of course the attendants on the boat were charmed. Not many of the hordes of tourists can say a single word. And so many of them think the empire never ended. The Bensons behaved like old India hands, and whenever Hugo Bloom did the opposite they looked down their horse-like noses at him.'

'My dear Tamara. What uncharacteristic zeal. And so unprofessional.'

'Well, if you had met them you'd know what I mean. So would whoever it was that you sent snooping around their place. Plenty of dirt to pick up there, in every sense of the word.'

Regular weekend parties were held at Fernley. Several of the paying guests had heard Hugo Bloom mention his snap decision to seek the Egyptian sunshine.

Everyone in the room (all of them ostensibly sketching or doing their embroidery with unbroken concentration) expected one of John Benson's unpredictable anathemas. 'I cannot bear women with streaked hair,' he would announce, or 'giant pandas,' or 'people who read the *Financial Times*.' He never gave reasons or discussed his prejudices but when the prohibition issued in his high, refined drawl, it was immutable. Listeners would look at his and his sister's faces, alike in angles and in attitude, and know that whatever was named would henceforth be banned from Fernley; and because the Bensons were so special, so original, so perfect a survival from a world where taste and culture reigned, of which the Weekend Book and the Society for Italic Handwriting, the Omega workshops and the Sesame Club were symbols, because theirs was a world in which the carefully chosen details of daily life all added up to, quite simply, civilisation, their peculiarities were all acceptable.

Hugo Bloom had read every published word about the lives of the Bloomsbury group. He said that he cherished a vision of the good life led by the Woolfs at Rodmell and the Bells at Charleston. He thought that Fernley provided the closest contemporary approach and was humbly grateful that he could participate in it. He was both a benefactor (for his presents went far beyond mere politeness) and a customer.

John Benson dealt in small antiques (which he called bibelots) and Victorian genre paintings; a series of them temporarily adorned Fernley and were the focus of John's lectures to the paying guests.

When Hugo got back from his holiday he wanted to bring some American friends who might be in a position to do John a bit of good. John Benson's lip curled at the expression. 'Holiday? Are you going away?' he said.

Hugo Bloom was going to Egypt. He had retained fond memories of the place from his army days. ('I cannot bear people who talk about their military prowess,' John Benson sometimes said.)

'It will be difficult to appreciate the antiquities without your guidance,' Hugo complained.

'But they provide specialist lecturers,' Ann said, finding the small print in the glossy brochures Hugo had brought with him.

All the tour operators offered instruction for holiday-makers from Professor this or Doctor that. 'One wonders whether there are any dons left in our universities. The archaeology departments will be denuded,' John Benson said.

'This one looks lovely,' Ann said, pulling her knitted jacket more closely round her. She held out a picture of a cruise liner with a swimming pool on the top deck surrounded by sun worshippers on reclining chairs.

'I could not bear the thought of a gin palace on the Nile,' John exclaimed, his fastidious hands turning over the photographs of temples, pyramids, death masks and tourists on camels.

'I wonder what made you think of Egypt, Hugo? Why not China? Porcelain . . . silk . . . the terracotta army . . .' Ann rose to wipe some dangling cobwebs from a cornice. Hugo, who had arrived unexpectedly, had found everyone gathered in what was once the servants' hall where they could huddle over a small cast-iron stove. The drawing room was decorated, though not heated, by a polished steel basket grate. Hugo had not offered to instal central heating. The Bensons wished he would.

'Hieroglyphics and temples. A little monotonous perhaps,' John Benson remarked.

'Not if we see things other tourists never get to.'

'I could not bear to be regarded as a tourist.'

'One hardly would be, in so small a party. Oh, John, couldn't we— '

Hugo Bloom said, 'This is a particularly expensive package, Ann.'

'I cannot bear people who imply that we are paupers,' John Benson said.

'My dear chap, I had no such— '

'Now that I read the brochure in detail, I must admit that it sounds quite attractive.'

'Yes, doesn't it,' Ann burst out. 'It even has Max Solomon as its courier.'

'If he speaks as obscenely as he writes you wouldn't care for him, Ann,' John said.

'I have seen him on television. He sounds wonderful,' Ann said mutinously.

'I can't imagine that it would really suit you. It will be quite arduous, especially this extra excursion to see Giles Needham's excavations in Lake Nasser,' Hugo said.

'Nasser!' John Benson might have been mentioning Hitler. He picked up the pamphlet again, turning the pages in his long, slightly dirty fingers. It was printed on cream paper, matt not shiny, in thermographically raised, elegantly classical type. It was illustrated with a Roberts print of Karnak. It was not designed to appeal to the mass market.

'I don't see why you and I shouldn't have the same little excitements in our lives as Hugo.'

'But John, it's so dear!'

'I cannot bear it when you always talk about money. Whatever Hugo may suppose, we are not completely destitute.'

'But John,' Ann began, before he went on:

'Our grandmother spent a winter at Aswan for her health.'

The discouraged hissing of damp logs in a stove designed for dry pinewood was all that could be heard as Ann Benson and Hugo Bloom waited for John to pronounce.

5

I must repeatedly remind myself that all humans are unique. Behaviour on holiday is so predictable as to make me doubt it. I deal with the usual demands and queries. I express gratification at the usual compliments. I feel the usual sentiments myself, at the sight of the sun setting behind the rosy Theban Mountain across the metallic, implacable flow of the Nile. Dancers are rehearsing a modern ballet in the ancient Temple of Luxor beside which we are moored. Most of the passengers complain of the loud, discordant music. I observe that Mr Knipe stands entranced by glimpses of leg and leotard between the massive columns.

Another early start, because privacy is what Osmond's customers are paying for.

At the Colossi of Memnon several people are moved to quote Shelley. 'My name is Ozymandias, king of kings: Look on my works ye Mighty, and despair.'

Mr Benson cannot bear people who utter incomplete tags. He declaims, 'Nothing beside remains. Round the decay of that colossal wreck, boundless and bare, the lone and level sands stretch far away.'

But the Colossi are not standing on lone and level sands. When I first saw them they rose as portents from fields of emerald alfalfa. Now there is a levelled patch of ground trodden naked around them. The doctor's wife has climbed the plinth to stand and be photographed where Ruth once stood.

On to the Ramasseum, the Valley of the Kings and the Temple of Hatshepsut. At the Tombs of the Nobles we must await our turn to enter. The desert valley is like a furnace, and we wonder how anyone can bear to live in such heat. Sayeed tells us that the government has tried to rehouse the residents in a village with all modern conveniences but they are hereditary tomb robbers and must stay near the source of their wealth.

'What can there be left to steal?' he is asked.

'When they can't find antiquities they fake them. Statuettes, scarabs . . .' Any antiquities we are offered for sale will be forgeries, Sayeed asserts, not for the first time.

'We all know that there is money in faking, don't we?' Vanessa Papillon says. 'I am sure John Benson can confirm it.'

'I have no sympathy with anyone who buys art for investment,' Timothy Knipe says. 'Serve them right if they are caught out by fakes.'

'The peasants make scarabs and feed them to turkeys. When the animal excretes them they look ancient,' Sayeed says.

He leads the way down into the tomb, where he shines his flashlight onto the brilliant frescoes. Purple grapes, thousands of years old, bloom on the ceiling. Sayeed speaks of the daily life and the eternal longings of the civil servant whose remains were interred here. The ladies in our party are enchanted by the pretty details. 'What wonderful colours, so well preserved.' One of them vows to redecorate her house on its design.

'The terracotta, the ochre,' she exclaims. 'With touches of turquoise. It will be empire style.'

'Pharaonic?' Vanessa asks, and is told Napoleonic. This country gives the least likely of us delusions of grandeur.

*

Max Solomon wrote of Tamara again at Kom Ombo, where the river steamer had moored in a beautiful place beside what smelt like a sewage farm. He described the Ptolemaic temple, and likened it to a post-reformation cathedral in England; he quoted without comment John Benson's praise of the beauty of Liverpool and Truro cathedrals, and Timothy Knipe's deprecation of their self-conscious archaism. Our new lecturer is a success, he added. She speaks clearly and uses witty contemporary analogies to enlighten the past of which she tells us. She makes the notes that Professor Thomas lent her sound like her own words.

'It was not as easy as all that,' Tamara said. 'I really had to slave at the Egyptology in private without letting the pax see me.'

'Pax?'

'It's what people in the holiday trade call passengers. Didn't you know?'

'You have learnt a good deal on this assignment that I am never likely to know,' Mr Black said. 'My only sight of the Nile was during the war. Not the best circumstances.'

'I can't believe it has changed.'

What Tamara had seen was like a vision of the past she had studied and tried to imagine. As the steamer moved southwards from Cairo it seemed to move backwards from the twentieth century. Laid out on either side was the immemorial pattern of riparian life. Women in orange, magenta, lime-green or vermilion robes clustered with their flat copper bowls to wash their clothes, crocks and children. Blindfold donkeys turned water-wheels. Small girls herded goats, boys drove donkeys, biblical patriarchs directed agrarian operations unsullied by machinery.

Wherever the boat was moored, its party of Europeans would set off to see temples or the traces of early habitations.

'I was nervous after that fright I had at Dendera,' Tamara said. 'I thought that Janet might escape while I was droning about dynasties.'

Janet had signed on for a day trip by bus across the eastern desert to the Red Sea – four hours' bumpy drive in each direction. But she had an acute attack of diarrhoea and was unable to join the twenty energetic characters who chose the discomfort.

'Lucky,' Tamara said. 'I was stuck with a scheduled lecture to the rest of them. I had visions of her hitching away on a boat or something.'

'What did you use? Ipecacuanha or something?'

'I'd found some castor oil in the doctor's bag. The salads of cooked vegetables tasted pretty odd anyway, and of course we were all being careful to keep off the raw stuff.'

'A risk?'

'What would you have done? Though you're right, of course, and I doubt whether the anxiety was justified at the time.'

Janet Macmillan had calmly followed the guides, listening to what they said with apparent attention. Her former lover seemed unembarrassed by her presence. It may be that Janet had hoped to upset Vanessa who, however, thrived on competitions that she won, and was ostentatiously possessive of the man who had once been the other woman's.

'Would you have sent me if you had thought she was in the role of the woman scorned rather than the scientist muzzled?' Tamara said.

'Possibly not,' Mr Black said. 'But we did not have enough information at the time. It seemed on the cards that Janet Macmillan was planning to get herself and her information away from us. It seemed to my masters that you could be relied on to prevent it, at a cheaper price than putting her under any other restraint. In any currency.'

Tamara said, 'By the time we got to Aswan I'd become convinced that her reason for coming on the trip had simply been to follow Timothy Knipe and make him suffer a bit. But she was beginning not to care. The sun and the beauty were calming her down.'

'Perhaps she had simply realised what a light-minded fellow he was,' Mr Black suggested. 'Max Solomon noticed it at once.'

February 7.

Our poet is beginning to make eyes at the other dottoressa, Tamara Hoyland. Indeed, were it not for my own age, I would do so too. The butterfly's undeniable beauty is of the type to shine in electric light in sophisticated surroundings. It does not suit her to be casual or windswept. Her clothes look as though she were modelling them for a magazine feature on suitable attire for the tropics. They seem faintly absurd, but she wears them with supreme self-confidence, despising other women's attempts at elegance. Miss Benson spends hours up on deck in what was once called a sun-suit. It is sleeveless and low cut, with a short skirt like a skater's, from which her mottled legs, dimpled like an orange skin, extend. Vanessa watches her with a kind of greedy disgust. Tamara Hoyland's clothes contain expensive labels. I have seen them on the garments flung on the ground when she bathes in the sun. But she wears them as though they were work gear. She puts on nothingness (but for three triangles of fabric) like a coronation robe. Even the crew, inured in spite of their religious prohibitions to the immodesty of European women, look at her as they pad across the deck. I have acquired a galabieh like theirs. It is comfortable and cool. It conceals my ageing flesh.

The butterfly is ailing. She has contracted a throat ailment and, *mirabile dictu*, is silent. Her voice is insured for six figures, she has whispered, a final statement. Her man is not assiduous in his attentions to her. He pads around the deck with a camera, telefoto lens attached, protruding like a phallus below his waist. A name, not his, is woven into the fabric of its long strap, like a dog's.

In the afternoon we arrive at the southernmost point of our boat's journey. The valley closes in upon the river. Here was the farthest corner of the Roman Empire. Here the poet Juvenal was posted to guard the boundaries of the regime he had mocked. We have seen enough, today and in the preceding days, to exhaust anyone other than an English country woman, but several of my party sally forth as soon as they have found their rooms in the hotel to look at Aswan's curiously municipal flowers. Some of the women have gone out with bare arms and shoulders and low-cut dresses, and the women in the Nubian village spit at them.

Hugo Bloom is seen coming out of a house in the town. 'Dr Hoyland and I saw you,' Lady Gentle insists. 'I am sure it was you. In Sharia el Suq, just beside the shop where they sell ebony models of feluccas. Do you have friends here, of all places?' He says he has been shopping, and displays a trophy, a brass tray. 'You weren't carrying a parcel,' Lady Gentle says. 'Perhaps you have found a lady friend. This is a man's country.'

After midnight I am woken by Mr Benson. He has ignored the warning (in words and drawings) about mosquitoes and opened his window onto the Nile. Now he is being dive-bombed by vicious insects. He expects the courier to change rooms with him.

I am dive-bombed by mosquitoes. Wakeful, I find the books Benson has left by his bed untempting. They are a monograph on Victorian watercolours and a directory of painters. The names of some of the more obscure are underlined.

I turn on the television and watch *The Red Shoes*, dubbed into Arabic.

February 8.

Topics of conversation: electric hair-dryers, diarrhoea and its reverse which is always more worrying for the British; the birds of the Nile.

Miss Benson finally expresses what her speaking glances have implied. 'Oh, Mr Solomon, we are so lucky to have someone of your eminence to travel with us.'

Miss Papillon has saved up less emollient remarks. She said, 'You are Jonty's father, aren't you?'

I had supposed that she had not made the connection. She goes on, 'He stood in for me once. It didn't work.'

Television and literature appeal alike to a fickle public. Both depend on luck.

Jonty has not been as lucky as Vanessa Papillon.

All the same, there is something fascinating about the woman. In her company, other people seem less interesting. She does not converse, she interrogates. Bemused by the magic of her attention, her victims reply. She has found out everything about her travelling companions though none of us can really interest her. The need to know is her professional deformity.

Jonty could do what she does and do it without making himself hateful. He would still be a human being. She is not.

I am sitting on the verandah with the doctor's wife and Miss Benson when a skeletal horse is whipped past us. They cry out in chorus: one 'ooh' in pity and anguish, the other 'oi' in an angry bark. They suffer more at the sight of the animals here than from the thin children with flies on their sticky eyelids.

My charges, like the human race, are divided into performers and watchers. I wonder whether the watchers are aware that they are not themselves the stars in their own stories.

My own habit, naturally and professionally, is to observe. Our butterfly is a good example of the centre-of-attraction type. She knows it. All she says and does is for show. She is an artefact.

Is that what I want for Jonty? He told me once that he would sell his soul for his own programme. He has little hope of achieving one so long as he remains in Vanessa's shadow.

I move to sit under a jacaranda tree. She comes to sit beside me. She is cute and canny, on the ball, street-wise; superficial, contemporary qualities. She is admirable in a way.

She says, 'It must be five years since you published anything. Why?' I do not reply, and she continues, 'Pining for your wife, I suppose. Work is the best remedy, you know.'

Work is the best remedy. I know. If I were a navvy or a doctor I would work. But I cannot work unless I feel. I dare not feel. When I work, I dream. I dare not dream.

She says, 'I don't know why you aren't better known.'

I think of the American research students who study my use of the semi-colon, of the libraries that compete for my archives.

She says, 'It isn't as though you haven't tried. Your agent wanted me to have you on the show.'

I had said at the time that it was ill-advised. Neither my work nor my personality lend themselves to being pushed by glossy young ladies in slick city suits, nor do I require synthetic fame derived from appearing on chat shows and attending literary lunches. I was a disappointment to the public relations person.

Vanessa takes a bottle of crimson varnish from her bag and begins to paint her nails. They are long, pointed, curved slightly inwards; predatory claws. I turn my eyes to the feluccas that sweep across the blue water. Between them are miniature craft made by the small boys who crouch in them and paddle with their hands. Well prepared tourists, like those who travel with Camisis, have come supplied with ball-point pens to give them.

'Jonty is rather like you,' Vanessa said.

'He is usually thought to resemble his mother.'

'I meant in character. Not enough get-up-and-go.' She means that my boy does not trample aside anyone who stands in his path. She means that he will get on in his chosen profession against her opposition; over her dead body. That is what she means.

6

Tamara had put on what seemed to be a convincing pretence of taking for granted the sites that struck the other first-time visitors with awe; and her careful plan-reading and preparation had enabled her to walk around even the stupendous Karnak with every appearance of already knowing her way. This enforced, hasty familiarisation with the archaeology of ancient Egypt had given her an affection for a period which had never seemed appealing before. 'They were really just like us,' Miss Benson insisted, and it did not seem quite as silly a remark as it would once have done. The surviving evidence of domestic life was endearing; and the monuments no more megalomaniac than the Louvre or Whitehall would seem when their ruins represented our times to future generations.

She wondered whether it would be apparent to the archaeologists who one day studied the twentieth century that the Temple of Abu Simbel, still staggering in its complex immensity, was a reconstruction. The reports and pictures of the work that had been done to save the monument were of an endeavour as intemperate, as ambitious, as the original building of all these reminders of slavery. She left the hotel at Aswan not expecting to like what she was to see.

February 10.

We wake to high wind (though I think that it is never calm here) and a haze over the sun. The hotel staff speak of dust storms and the khamsin. The hot wind from the south may ground flights. The creation of the lake has changed the climate.

All but three of the party have signed on for the daytrip to Abu Simbel. Eight of us are to go on from there to Qasr Samaan.

We are driven to the unpleasant airport in Aswan. The doctor plays his radio so that we can all hear the World Service news. He tells us to make the most of it, before the eight of us set off into the middle of nowhere.

The princess is still missing, and famine still rages in Africa only a small distance, on the continental scale, from where we are now.

'Why can't they just send the food and get her back?' one of the women asks.

'A very sentimental solution,' John Benson says.

'It's such a good cause. Like Robin Hood.'

'Famine is nature's way of limiting the world's population,' Benson replies, through a mouth full of the sandwiches with which our hotel has supplied us.

'You often hear well–fed people say that,' remarks Vanessa. 'Just as you hear healthy young people say that it's a good thing if we don't all live to clutter up the geriatric wards.'

She's right; but the analogy I think of is the reincarnations conversation, which has been gone through more than once since our arrival in this country. Vanessa thinks she might have been Cleopatra. In our imaginations, starvation, sickness and inferior social positions are someone else's fate.

We wait; and wait. The aircraft is coming. It is not

coming. It comes. It will not take off again. It will take off again. Eventually it takes off, a small craft filled with camera-slung tourists.

Lake Nasser is like a huge oil slick on the sea of desert. Its colours are viscous. The land is hostile, barren. 'How strange, how frightening,' the passengers murmur.

The pilot makes the aeroplane swoop to and fro, to gasps and squeals. The statues are not so impressive from the air and we land at a small, prosaic airstrip. But when we round the artificial mounds built to support the re-sited temple we all gasp at the size of the quadruplicate monarchs. The Colossi of Ramasses warn of Egypt's might, those of Nefertiti welcome visitors to its civilisation. Miss Benson quotes Shelley again.

One cannot help being awed by the grandeur of the worked stone. But our awe is scientific not mystical. We are almost more impressed by the feats of engineering that moved the temples than by the ancient art that built them.

Abu Simbel is no longer numinous. The dust of ages does not lie beneath our feet.

'They should have brought the potsherds,' Hugo Bloom rightly says; at other temples the visitor walks on a carpet of the centuries' debris.

One can tell that Tamara Hoyland is the sort of person who passes examinations after brief revision to the fury of those who have to slave for three terms. She listens knowledgeably to Sayeed and can answer questions that are addressed to her. But she confides to me that she is counting on filling in the gaps with Giles Needham at Qasr Samaan. Those of us who are to venture further into what once was Nubia (an ill-assorted party, I must say) are reminded how the vast likenesses of Ramasses and his Nefertiti once gave warning to travellers between the two lands.

'I think it is quite creepy,' Miss Benson says. 'I feel premonitions.'

'Of what?' Timothy Knipe asks. He is the kind of person to read runes, or palms, or entrails.

'I don't know.'

'Are you a psychic?'

'What nonsense,' her brother interrupts.

'Don't you believe in Pharaoh's curses?' says Vanessa Papillon.

'You can hardly expect me to take such a question seriously.'

'Vanessa's too down-to-earth for that kind of thing,' Timothy Knipe says. He does not seem to admire the attribute. Later I hear them quarrel.

I drink mango juice. Timothy Knipe says that his beer is flat and warm. Vanessa tells him that he will have the right to complain on the day that he picks up the bill. He says that is typical of her materialistic attitude. He thinks that she thinks she has bought him.

I am joined by the courier from another party of Britons.

We agree on the curious infantilism of our charges, who surrender their adult independence on this kind of holiday, and who, bent on pleasure, lack patience and philosophy as they did when they were children.

'They want to be nannied,' my acquaintance says. 'Mine expect me to tell them when to get up in the morning and what to wear.' I explain the Camisis arrangement with Giles Needham. He is interested in the economics of so small a party's travel, and whistles soundlessly when I tell him how much my charges have paid. 'All that to sit in a sandstorm in a reservoir!' he says.

Osmond is proud of having offered a unique extra to his Egyptian package. He has contributed to the cost of the excavations at Qasr Samaan and in exchange his clients will be welcomed there. His generosity will be acknowledged in the report, and exclusive photographs will appear in his next brochure.

But Needham left England last October. There has been no contact since. I hope he will be reliable.

He is reliable. Just in time for its passengers to take our places on the return flight to Aswan, a tug-boat from Qasr Samaan approaches across choppy water. Five sunburnt Europeans and three Egyptians in European clothes leap from it and dash past us. They are followed by several dark-skinned men in native dress.

'Have fun,' one calls, and another says, 'Keep our places warm.' They are to have a three-day break from work while we use their facilities. They look healthy, dusty, a little wild-eyed. The fleshpots of Aswan beckon them. We watch the plane, containing them and the rest of the Camisis party, circle once more around the island before turning northwards. We (or at least I) feel curiously abandoned. We are south of the Tropic of Cancer.

We sit on the rock to watch the tug being loaded with supplies. The crew are all Nubians, with dark round faces. They take aboard crates of oranges and bananas, tomatoes and tinned milk. John Benson watches with disapproval.

'Why they need so many men . . .' Certainly far more are at work than would seem necessary at home. A patriarchal figure in white draperies is directing it. Beside him another, captain or pilot, sits cross-legged, motionless, in the bows.

At last we embark. We wait on board while the frenzy continues. My charges are impatient. I refuse to see if there is anything I can do.

After another hour we move slowly out onto the water to hoarse shouts from the patriarch. Beneath us is the bed of the narrow Nile and the sandstone cliffs against which the Colossi of Abu Simbel once loomed. The water is deep over the drowned land. We see nothing through it, but where dry rocks once spread for endless miles points of sparkling light wink from wave to wave.

The tug is crewed by about a dozen men. It is flat bottomed and an awning flaps over a section of the stern. We sit under the canvas, and the women of the party anoint themselves against the reflected light. I ask in English, French and Italian how long the journey to Qasr Samaan will take but cannot understand the voluble reply.

Tamara said, 'I understood. They were saying that it was in the lap of God. I thought it was a rather sinister answer. But the whole place was sinister, actually.'

'That's what Max Solomon thought too.'

We remain within sight of the lake-shore which is stone, all greyish brown. I have seen many desolate landscapes. This is not the most forbidding of all, because the water redeems it; but it is empty and dead where the new shore meets the new sea. If this penned-up water bursts its high dam it would flood the length of the Nile and inundate Cairo. A bomb could breach the dam.

The tug has a diesel engine, whose fumes blow back onto us in the strong wind. John Benson says he cannot bear the smell. 'It is the stink of civilisation. I had hoped to leave that behind.'

The water is choppy. Miss Benson lies prone on the deck, her eyes closed.

'Somehow one wouldn't expect to be seasick in Egypt,' Hugo Bloom murmurs. He is happy. His skin, naturally dark, is deeply tanned. He wears army shorts and a rolled-sleeve shirt. He looks like an Israeli soldier/scholar. He gazes ahead with eager eyes, his teeth biting around his pipe. He has been excited by everything we have seen and is one of the few people among us whose pleasure shows. I wonder about the motives of some of our party. Their holiday is expensive and some of it is arduous. Why are they here?

After about three hours the blank expanse of water is interrupted by a low mound ahead. The rays of the lowering sun shine on white stones and columns. The patriarch shouts, the wheel is turned, the engine dies. Soon it appears that it was not intended to. The sailors rush about, their bare feet slapping against the wooden deck, and we realise that they are agitated. We are drifting away from the island, north. We perceive people on the island. They seem excited too. We listen to the sound of an engine refusing to start.

'Can't you do something?' Vanessa Papillon says. She has draped her head and neck in gauzy scarves and wears impenetrable glasses. I can see Janet Macmillan reflected in them.

'Anybody understand engines?' John Benson says, since it is obvious that he does not.

I do not worry. I say that we are hardly likely to drown.

We don't drown. Eventually some poles are produced. We are paddled towards Qasr Samaan. There is just enough daylight left for us to see the way to step on shore.

7

'I had this feeling of foreboding,' Tamara said.

'Hindsight.'

'No, I really did. I noticed it because I'm not the kind of person who feels vibes and shivers. We were being handed across a kind of plank, to step onto the island, and that silly Ann Benson said something so acute that I stumbled and the Nubian whose hand was on my arm gripped me so hard that I got a bruise.'

'Ann Benson?'

'She said I'd be able to take my eye off Janet now we were marooned here, and so would Hugo Bloom.'

'What did she mean?'

'That's what I said. And she got sort of fluttery and muttered something about us both seeming so fascinated by her. And then I . . . well, I came over queer, as they say. The heat, probably, or the beginning of that tummy upset. But I remember thinking that I really didn't want to get into the barge where we were to live. I can't explain it.'

'Our chronicler does not seem to have had any similar experience.'

We are conducted by smiling Nubians – mem. Saki's little Nubian boy; these coal black, white-toothed young men are equally charming – into a barge that is moored on the western side of this island. It will be our home for two days.

Giles Needham is there to greet us. His face is familiar from the television screen. He is very tall, stooping, with perfect teeth, green eyes and clear brown skin. He bowls over not only Mr and Miss Benson – oh dear – but also our butterfly, who flutters. She reminds him that they have spoken on the telephone. 'The only man who ever refused to come into my net!' she tells us.

'I had to get back here, as far as I recall,' he says.

'You could have made time for me. You will next season, now that we have met.' She puts her hand on his, and looks confidingly up through her long, thick eyelashes. He draws away.

One other European has remained here to entertain the Camisis party. It is a girl student called Polly. I observe Vanessa's narrow examination of her, and a satisfied nod; an 'I thought as much' expression.

All the rest of the archaeological party has gone to Aswan for 'rest and recreation' while we are here. So has the doctor and the government inspector whose role is to prevent foreign excavators from making off with Egyptian property.

We are shown to the beds vacated by them all. There are ten cabins on the lower deck. Each is identically furnished with a narrow bed made of palm leaves stretched between acacia wood frames and an article of furniture known as an angareeb that can be used both as table and as storage cupboard. My cubicle also has a locked trunk, the property of Needham's assistant, which he has covered with a length of locally woven cotton. Above his bed he has fastened a photograph of a pleasant, messy woman with two small children. A mosquito net dangles from the ceiling.

There are two cubicles (each containing a wc and a sink – no shower or bath) for which we queue.

The facilities are not luxurious. I expect complaints from at least two members of my party.

On the way upstairs to the living deck where we are to assemble for drinks, I receive the first grumbles. I need hardly add that they are from John Benson. He wishes me to arrange for the removal of some photographs that belong to the finds conservator who usually sleeps there. I peer in. They are of beautiful and nubile girls.

The living deck is a long, low room, where a narrow table is just big enough for the whole party to sit on two benches for meals and a few canvas chairs are scattered for relaxation. Cooking is done in the other barge, where the workmen and stewards live. The flat roof is for the excavation work; it is used for sorting and photographing finds and they call it the 'Pot Deck'.

Our presence for two days seems to me a high price for Giles Needham to pay for Camisis's financial contribution. He says that they always take a break from work half way through the season in any case and that he does not regret the fleshpots of Aswan. He says that in funding the excavation, every little helps. He offers us whisky, Omar Khayyam wine and mineral water, which is the chief item is luggage that comes here. A mini-pyramid of crates is stacked on the shore. Lake Nasser looked very clear and Hugo Bloom says something about coals to Newcastle, but I reiterate my courier's warning about always using bottled water.

I don't wish to be responsible for pax with gut trouble here.

The barge is lit by few, faint bulbs. There is an electricity generator. It is not powerful enough for fires. Vanessa complains of the cold, with some justification. It is remarkable how the temperature drops once the sun is down. She sends Tim Knipe to fetch her shawl, a cloud of raspberry pink mohair.

Dinner consists of chops, rice and tomatoes.

'Fresh meat and veg,' Giles Needham exclaims, tucking in. 'We only get that when the tug comes.'

The tug goes to Abu Simbel every three weeks. Otherwise the excavators and their staff live on tinned food, rice and cereals. Sometimes the workmen catch fish.

'You'll get scurvy,' Miss Benson says.

'We take vitamin tablets, don't we, Polly?' Giles Needham speaks to the girl with absent-minded kindness as he might to a kitten.

'We look all right though, don't we?' she says, holding out her narrow, round arm and admiring it; a Narcissus. 'Oh,' she wails, 'I have chipped a nail. Look!'

Nobody looks.

Vanessa is perpetually inquisitive. She cross-examines Giles Needham about the arrangements. 'You mean to say that really you are all marooned here?'

'Us and the workmen.'

'Where do they come from?'

'They are fishermen. They lived here until it was all flooded. The government tried to resettle them all on the Nile, further north, but they pine for home. Some of them live in shanties on the lake-shore.'

'It's so barren here. What do they build them out of?' Hugo asks.

'Woven palm leaves.'

'Cold and uncomfortable,' Vanessa comments.

'That is one of our problems. They burn absolutely anything they can get hold of in the winter. We need new beds and angareebs every season.'

Vanessa is watching Polly. 'You weren't here last season?'

'No, I'm new here. I came after Christmas.' Her voice is husky and its accent very Knightsbridge. Her hair is loose and falls across her face. She looks like fifty thousand other rich little English girls wallowing in the dirt their nannies forbade.

'Are you a student? What about your university term?'

Giles Needham stands up. He has to bend either his knees or his back if his head is not to scrape the ceiling. He manages to suggest without commanding that we should all call it a day. There does not seem to be anything else to do.

I have been writing by the light of a kerosene lamp, since the generator was turned off. I rest my notebook on the angareeb. I am unexpectedly comfortable. I hear voices in conversation; the slap of bare feet on the deck above my head; the flap of the awning over the pot deck. My sleeping tablets are on the table beside the mineral water. For once I feel as though I shall not need them.

Natural sleep is slow to come. I lie in the dark and woo it.

There is a small window above my head. I can see the brilliant stars, as different from England's puny twinkles as is electric light from a single candle.

Tamara said, 'He must have fallen asleep quite fast, though, because he didn't write about the row between Janet and Timothy.'

'You heard one?'

'I should think everyone must have done. I was in the cabin next to hers and caught every word. I could even hear the sound of her getting undressed. And then Timothy Knipe came in. He did begin in a whisper, but he didn't keep it up. They were quarrelling about Janet being there at all. He said she was following him around, and how dared she spoil his first trip to Egypt by having her beady eyes on him the whole time.'

She said she had as much right to buy a package holiday as he had. 'We used to share our interest in Egyptology.'

'You had never even heard of it until you met me,' he said.

'You must be a better teacher than you thought. Maybe you could earn your living that way, when you run out of women to support you.'

'I might have known you'd talk about money,' he said.

'No doubt it is a matter of indifference to your new meal ticket.'

'You leave Vanessa out of this.'

'Oh, willingly. Out of everything.'

Tim Knipe sneered; it was the only word for his tone. If Tamara had been in Janet Macmillan's place she would have hit him. 'Poor Janet, devoured by jealousy. The only deadly sin that carries no pleasure in the committing. You can't hurt me, or Vanessa. You are beneath her attention.'

'Are you telling me that she doesn't know we lived together for two years? That we were going to get married? I wonder whether she'll give half her salary to your kids, the way I did? You are going to be sorry you chucked me, Timothy.'

'You are pathetic. I suppose you are here in order to make me and Vanessa uncomfortable.'

'I came because I wanted to see Egypt. And Qasr Samaan, after Giles's programmes about it. I don't give a damn if you are here at the same time with your new owner. Anyone who buys a gigolo knows he's on sale to the highest bidder.'

'Oh good. That's just as well. You're bound to hear me and Vanessa together as her cabin is next to yours.'

'In that case she'll know about me if she didn't already.' She raised her voice. 'Are you listening, Vanessa? Have your property back. But take my word for it, he isn't worth the money.'

Everyone must have heard Tim flouncing out; and, unfortunately for her, Janet's muffled sobs.

The exchange had sounded convincing. But Tamara found herself vividly reminded of the situation Agatha Christie had presented in *Death on the Nile*. Was it possible that Janet and Tim were putting on a show? And if so, whatever for?

Max Solomon wrote:

I slept, but badly.

Half-conscious, I heard conversations. Asleep, I dreamt.

I dread my dreams. Once I could neutralise them by making fiction of them. They were my raw material. Now I dream and there is no consolation. Trains thunder through my imagination. There are uniforms. There is—

No. No more. Tonight I shall take a double dose of barbiturates. Then at least I shall not remember the nightmares.

Vanessa Papillon says she had a sleepless night. I am not sure whether it is a complaint or a boast. John Benson was disturbed by other people's snores.

Breakfast is coffee, ships' biscuits and tinned butter ennobled by Oxford marmalade. We are assured that the coffee was made from mineral water.

In daylight we see that the living room is a pleasant, wood-lined saloon. Giles Needham says that it is really just camping. But it is the kind of camp that empire builders had, well maintained by respectful natives who pad in and out with the food, and clear plates away with a grace more suitable for a West End hotel.

'How cheerful they all look,' Ann Benson says.

'Remarkable considering that we are sitting above their villages.' Giles tells us what is lost under the vast lake. Nine thousand homes and nine hundred thousand palm trees were drowned in the Sudan. Now its people starve, and their sympathisers in a small country far away try to extort food for them by crime against our Pharaoh's relative. North of the border in Egypt, as many trees and homes again disappeared to less regret than the temples, monuments, and the Nubians' own traditional culture.

Qasr Samaan is very near the uncertain border between the two countries. We are more than five hundred kilometres from Aswan, sitting by a new island that was a mountain top. It is about two acres, roughly triangular.

Thirty kilometres north of us is Qasr Ibrim where the Egypt Exploration Society has been running excavations since long before it became an island. It was on the southern border of the Roman Empire. Then it became a Nubian bishopric, and later was occupied by mercenaries from Bosnia until only a century ago. A wealth of written material from all periods has been found. It is a richer site than Qasr Samaan, but Giles Needham's propaganda was for his own.

'Nobody suggested we could go there,' John Benson complains.

'That's my good fortune then,' Giles replies very pleasantly. 'I am looking forward to showing you our site here, and giving you a taste of life on the dig.'

'Just what we wanted,' Hugo Bloom says.

'We are working on the remains of a cathedral with some wonderful frescoes.'

'Christian?' Benson asks.

'Yes, Coptic of course. And we have the southernmost example of pharaonic material too. We are well beyond the boundary of the Egyptian empire.'

'Jewellery and gold?' Vanessa asks.

'Alas no. Pipe stems. Fragments of textile and bits of artillery. What about fetching the site plan, Poll, would you? We'll show everyone the layout.'

Hugo Bloom wonders who keeps the things that Needham finds.

As we have already heard from Sayeed, the Egyptian government is very keen to prevent any antiquities from being exported. That's why an inspector from the state antiquities service is stationed here. The dig may not proceed without him.

It has seemed a long day. The incessant wind becomes exhausting. Vanessa wears a hat fastened down by a long chiffon scarf that ties under her chin. Polly says:

'I think being windswept suits me.' From time to time she pulls a glass from her pocket to make sure of it.

We all become very dusty. Needham tells us not to worry; the servants will wash all our clothes. We see them washing their own, kneeling by the lake in traditional poses, their movements graceful and unforced as they slam the fabric against the rock, up and down, up and down, and then swirl it in the water. A line on their barge, fifty yards from ours, is festooned with blue, brown and white garments.

Miss Benson wishes she could swim here. Giles Needham often does. He says there is no bilharzia in the lake, except where it is stagnant. The water here is well enough agitated by the wind. It is not deep on this northern side of Qasr Samaan where the rock slopes away gently, but on the other side a cliff drops down to one hundred and fifty feet.

'What about crocodiles?' Miss Benson says.

'They say there are some,' Giles says, and Polly squeals:

'You never told me that.'

'You are unlikely to see any. But when one of the ferries to Wadi Halfa from Aswan went down a few years ago, all the passengers were eaten if they weren't drowned.' He has a ghoulish, satisfied smile; the adults among us disbelieve him.

We straggle across the rocks behind him to see his excavations.

Trenches outlined by string are dug into the dust. From them arise white and grey stones. They are the remains of the church. Needham shows us the frescoes. At first it looks as though only the eye of religious or archaeological faith could discern them but the ghost of multicoloured pictures gradually emerges. The remaining paint is pink, pale blue, faint beige. Once it was lapiz and azure, terracotta, ochre and gold. Giles runs his finger around outlines that were the Virgin and Child, St John and St Antony.

Tamara Hoyland is enthralled. She stoops to the trench, gazes up to the decorations, hangs on Needham's words.

The rest of us are more easily sated. We begin to wander across the island. It is uniformly grey, rocky and dusty. Across the water on the shore more dirt and stones run out of sight to north and south. There are no palm trees. There is no sign of present or past inhabitation. It is desolate; a wilderness. The only special feature is a row of rough rectangles cut into the side of the rock on the lake-shore. Polly says that they are the graves of the Roman soldiers who died here, beyond their frontier.

'Poor things,' she says. 'So far from home. So lonely. It's . . . it's rather creepy, don't you think?'

'Creepy?'

'They must have felt cut off from everything, like us. I might as well be on the moon. Or in prison or something.'

'You are kept busier,' I suggest.

'Yeah. Labelling bits of broken pottery with red and green ink.'

'You are sorry you came?'

'I wanted to work with Giles. He's so . . .' Her voice trails off. Even to a man who could be her grandfather, perhaps especially, she cannot utter the thoughts; I can guess them. He wild as a hawk, she soft as a dove. True love; and all the self-obsession that accompanies it. She never forgets herself for an instant, always looking in her little mirror, re-tying her headscarf, pulling at her skirt, touching the little blemishes on her face.

Polly is not a star, like Vanessa, not delicious like Tamara, not intellectual like Janet, nowhere near as intelligent as any of them – three remarkable women, after all – but she has the attraction that the young hold for us as we get older, of, simply youth – firm flesh, supple limbs, attributes that Polly will not learn to value herself until she has lost them. She probably agonises about her underslung jaw and close-set eyes.

My hat blows off, and she retrieves it for me. She says, 'This wind. It gets on your nerves, don't you think? The others say that awful things happen if you are out here too long. Do you think it could really make you mad?' I tell her about the wind variously known as the khamsin, meltemi, or mistral and how its influence can be accepted as an excuse for crime.

'Crimes of passion, yeah,' she says. 'I wonder what it would feel like if a man killed for me.' But no man would kill for Polly; nor for Ann Benson. I could see the other three women as femmes fatales; in their own ways, each could be a tragic heroine.

8

I have been sitting on the peak of the island watching my party. The Bensons poke discontentedly among the ruins. John will be saying that he cannot bear them. His sister will say that they are perfectly fascinating. Usually Hugo Bloom pacifies his friend but he has been lying in the sun in the windbreak of a rock with Janet Macmillan. I watch him sit up, and speak to her earnestly and at some length. He takes her by the arm. He seems to plead. Janet rolls over abruptly. She stands up, and makes an unmistakably negative gesture with her hand. She moves away.

'Very interesting,' Vanessa Papillon says. I had not noticed that she was standing so close to me. She goes on, 'That's the difference between me and amateurs like your son Jonathan. All he would have seen there is a man getting the sexual brush-off.'

'What did you see?' I ask.

'What a professional journalist who has useful sources and knows how to use them would see.' She smirks, like the other cats she resembles.

I shall advise Osmond that this part of the package should not be repeated next year. The place is too claustrophobic. We are thrown too much together.

I have never felt quite as I do here. The isolation makes me uneasy, even frightened. It is a kind of panic fear. There is no communication at all with the outside world. The expedition is self-sufficient, with its supplies of preserved foods and its own doctor. 'He gets very bored,' Giles Needham says.

After lunch (tinned tuna fish, peas and pears) most of us disperse to lie down out of the midday sun. Giles Needham works on – 'We always do a nine-hour day' – but since digging is suspended during the absence of the government inspector he is sorting finds on the pot deck.

I listen to the sounds of this curious environment. The water is naturally tideless but is blown into waves that slap against the sides of the barge; wind whistling into every corner; the flapping awning; the continuous clicking of sand or dirt against the deck and sides of the barge; the voices of the Nubian workmen. They never bring their wives, though some have gone away now to visit them. They earn enough in a season here to support their families for a year. They think themselves lucky in comparison with the rest of their dispossessed countrymen.

Hugo Bloom asked Giles why the Nubians don't use feluccas or other smaller boats on the lake. It seems they have no tradition of going on the water although the ancients garrisoned the Nile and had a fleet as far as it was navigable – which was about as far as where we are now. South of their patrols the Nile was obstructed by cataracts and ran through ravines. Now the water is navigable and ferries ply it between Wadi Halfa and Aswan. But for the poor inhabitants there is no wood left to make boats.

Perhaps it is because they have no tradition of sailing that the men are having trouble in mending the tug that brought us here. We were to spend the afternoon travelling further south, probably into the Sudan, to see some carved rock statues. The patriarch has explained to Giles that this is impossible. Even those of us who cannot understand the gutturals and fricatives of Arabic can read the sign language.

'Don't say we shall be stuck here tomorrow?' Vanessa protests, having evidently given up any hope of charming the impervious Giles. He regrets that she is so anxious to get away. She glances from him to Polly. 'You know how it is for us journalists. Never happy out of reach of a telephone.'

'But you are on holiday,' Miss Benson says.

'Nothing to report from here, surely,' Giles says.

Vanessa turns her tawny gaze on him. 'You'd be surprised. Or perhaps you wouldn't.'

John Benson sits in the awning's shade, ignoring the pots that are spread out beside him, and grumbles. Tamara Hoyland is still lying down. She ate little lunch. 'Cleopatra's revenge?' Vanessa said to her.

Hugo Bloom has gone with Polly to examine the facilities for taking and developing photographs. It is an important part of the work here, so much of which consists of recording what cannot be moved and may disappear. The cubicle, boarded in against the light and as hot as the black hole of Calcutta, contains an extraordinary assortment of chemicals and equipment.

'I cannot bear inefficiency,' John Benson says.

Vanessa, walking past him, says lightly, 'Even in the fine arts?' He watches her with dislike as she goes downstairs towards Tim Knipe's heroic snores. She is a dislikeable woman. She has told me at least a dozen times that I should be getting down to work. Can she suppose that I actually choose not to? Sometimes she speaks of Jonty. Her tone is slighting. But if it were not for her, Jonty would have his chance.

An under-occupied afternoon. My childlike charges should have been provided with entertainment, and resent going without. Giles Needham began to look harried. He will be glad to see us leave tomorrow.

Now we are all 'changing for dinner'. Both words are euphemisms. The tinned food will be served with vitamin supplements. Only one of us has brought a wardrobe that is capable of variation.

Somebody has diarrhoea. Somebody else has sinus trouble.

Vanessa Papillon sends Tim to fetch her a new bottle of mineral water. I hear him commenting to somebody else that its distributors must be making a fortune.

John Benson, in the cabin next to mine, is uninhibitedly farting.

Footsteps go up the stairs. Drinks are on offer in the saloon.

I hear rubber soles squeaking up the stairs. Ann Benson, in her sensible, if hot, brogues. The rest of them wear rope-soled shoes.

I shall go up now. I shall click up in my leather sandals. Who will recognise my tread?

Later. Shall I take the barbiturates against the dreams? Or shall I sleep naturally? My supply is running low. Vanessa Papillon 'borrowed' my spare bottle. I may have a greater need of them before I can get more. But the dreams!

I have left my party listening to a lecture by Giles Needham, who performs with the fire and vision that tempted so many of our party here in the first place. Polly hangs on every word. Vanessa went down to bed saying that she never listens to lectures. Tamara Hoyland did not come up for dinner. She is the first of us to succumb to the dreaded D and V.

I feel uneasy myself; not as to the digestion, but probably as a result of last night's dreams. They stay with me all day.

I shall take some pills later; when the others are in bed and my duties are done.

Someone is shouting.

Feet are thudding on the stairs. I

There, mid-phrase, the diary of Max Solomon ended.

His writing carried on, even on the same page, even on the same line, but it was of a different kind.

The journal had been in a considered prose style, in careful handwriting, as though the author were performing an exercise to keep his muscles supple; brainwork.

After the interruption the pen had raced across the page almost without punctuation, undisciplined. It was a gush of creation that would be published to the greatest acclaim of Max Solomon's career, and to astonished critical evaluation of the new style in which he had written. It was uninhibited, unmannered, a flood of truth. The book was titled *Refugee*. It began as it had begun in that exercise book. The first sentence read, '*The mother threw the boy away from the soldiers, out of the moving train.*'

9

When Tim Knipe screamed Tamara Hoyland was standing by the open door of her cabin with the fresh bottle of water. She crossed the passage to Vanessa's room. Tim moved further into it and she followed him, allowing the door to swing closed behind her.

Vanessa Papillon was sprawled on the bed with her arms flung above her head, and her legs, outlined by the sheet, widespread. Her mouth hung open. Her eyes stared. Vomit smeared her face and the pillow onto which it had fallen. Excrement stained the bedclothes.

The glass on the angareeb had been overturned. There was a quarter-full bottle of water beside it.

Tamara gently shoved Tim aside. She picked up the opened bottle of water, and replaced it with her own full one. Then she turned, and hit Timothy Knipe on each cheek in turn. She put all her strength behind the blows. The falsetto screaming stopped. He fell to his knees beside the bed.

'Well done,' Hugo Bloom said. He joined Tamara in the narrow space. The other members of the party were jammed in the doorway, craning to see in.

Max Solomon's face had turned grey. The lines under his eyes, deeply incised, outlined them as though with a kohl pencil. His mouth had fallen open, squared like the mask of tragedy. Ann Benson's underlip was caught in her teeth, her forehead crinkled in an intense frown. John Benson looked as though he was about to say that he could not bear people to die.

Janet Macmillan peered between their shoulders. Her face was intent, as it must be when she looked into a microscope; detached and scientific. Polly on the other hand was completely subjective in her reaction. She had buried her face in Giles Needham's shoulder. He absent-mindedly patted her back. Then he put her to one side and edged his way into the room. It was as though a director had demanded action.

Hugo Bloom said, 'How very macabre.' He twitched at the soiled sheet to pull it up over the dead woman's head.

Polly had begun to cry in whoops and gasps like a much younger child. Giles Needham said, 'She shouldn't be here. Could someone take her upstairs?'

'I'll give her one of my homeopathic potions.' Ann Benson assumed the mantle of efficiency. 'Come along, my dear.'

Max Solomon followed them, away from the death chamber, walking like an automaton.

'I suppose he is all right,' Giles said. 'He isn't a young man. The shock . . .'

Hugo Bloom followed the writer, and looked in through the door of his cabin. 'He's already scribbling.'

Tim Knipe wiped his face on the back of his hand. Moisture glistened on his beard. He said, 'Work is the artist's therapy.' He pushed past Tamara and the others and turned towards his own cabin. 'You have to write it out of you. It's the way to deal with your traumas.'

'I don't suppose any of you know about medicine?' Giles Needham said. 'I shouldn't have let our quack go off with the others.'

'My sister has her first-aid certificate,' John Benson said.

'We don't need a doctor to tell us Vanessa's dead,' Janet said, her voice high and shaking.

Hugo Bloom took her arm. He said, 'I have some valium.'

John Benson followed them up the stairs. Left alone with the corpse, Giles and Tamara glanced at each other. She thought about the dynamics of group organisation. Somebody was going to have to take charge, and it looked as though that somebody was going to be Giles if only because they were on his territory.

He picked up the fallen glass and carefully put it exactly on the damp ring it had earlier left on the table top.

'I'm not sure what happens next,' he said.

'We get out of here and shut the door,' she replied.

'Yes of course. The smell . . .'

Someone was being sick in one of the lavatory cubicles. It was John Benson; he interspersed his spasms with imprecations. Tamara realised that the emergency had settled her own stomach; a drastic cure.

'Let's go on deck. Some fresh air . . .' she said. Giles followed her up the two narrow flights of stairs. The others were huddled in the saloon. Up on deck the wind blew the clinging odours from her, and replaced it with the acrid smell of the workmen's dung fires and the food they grilled on them.

'I wonder what the formalities will be,' Tamara said.

'God knows. Do the Egyptians have coroners and inquests, would you suppose? And post mortems and— ?' He halted, shocked by his train of thought. 'I suppose it was a natural death.'

'Natural?' Tamara said, thinking of the anguished, filthy figure down below.

'I mean . . . nobody else involved.'

'She could have taken too many sleeping pills.'

'Suicide?'

'Or accident. This was on the floor.' Tamara held out a small plastic container. In the erratic light of the one kerosene lantern, Giles read the label.

'Seconal, one to be taken at – but these are Max Solomon's. Were they in her room?'

'I should think Vanessa helped herself to them.'

'I wouldn't put it past her.' His voice trailed away. 'Sorry. That sounded pretty tasteless.'

'There's no denying that it is the sort of thing she'd do.'

'But not taking too many on purpose?'

'I hardly knew her any better than you,' Tamara said. 'Less well probably. I did not interest her.'

'I only wish I hadn't. Then she'd never have come here in the first place.'

'The penalty of fame.'

'Fame!' Giles sounded embarrassed. 'That wasn't why. She was famous enough not to need me. Oh God, I'm making it sound even worse. What I mean is, I made a temporary hit with those TV programmes. It seemed to be what people were in the mood for. But fame like that is easy come, easy go, and I never wanted it anyway. All I did it for was to raise some money for another season here. You know how difficult it is to get archaeology properly funded nowadays.'

'I do indeed,' Tamara agreed.

'I mean, I didn't take Vanessa seriously. She asked me on her silly show and I obviously wasn't interested. But she simply wouldn't give up.'

'I don't suppose she was used to being turned down.'

'So it seemed. She took it as some sort of personal affront. She . . . well, honestly, she pursued me.'

'And you think that's why she came on the Camisis tour?'

'I'd guess so. There are plenty of others to choose from. Swans, Bales, Serenissima . . . it's not as though she was interested in what we are doing here, and you really need to be, to put up with the conditions. Or so some of your party have been telling me, in no uncertain terms.'

'Yes,' Tamara said thoughtfully. 'And they were warned.

The brochure was very explicit about it. Step out of the twentieth century to Qasr Samaan, and don't expect twentieth-century amenities. Vanessa must have known what she'd find here.'

'Yes. Me.'

'It sounds a bit exaggerated,' Tamara said, though she could understand a woman going overboard for this man.

'Well, so it was. She was. I've never met anyone so exaggerated. She simply wasn't used to not getting what she wanted, and she wanted me. I'm sorry, Tamara, it isn't the sort of thing one ought to say or even think, but if you'd heard her . . . She cornered me last night.'

'How did she manage it? There isn't much privacy.'

'Everyone else had turned in already. Tim was talking to Janet Macmillan. They were having some sort of row, you could hear him shouting from up here.'

'Oh yes. I heard that.'

'You couldn't have avoided it. Anyway, I was up here having a sly smoke.' Giles tamped down his tobacco and struck a match. He sucked in a draught of soothing nicotine, and said, 'I thought some of your party would make a fuss if I lit up down there. My own colleagues don't like it either. So I've got into the habit of coming on deck last thing. And Vanessa came up after me and . . .'

'Made a pass at you?'

'That's putting it mildly. She was making the sort of offer it is embarrassing to refuse.'

'But you did refuse?'

'We were interrupted before I had to.'

'Polly?'

'Yes.'

'I expect she was jealous of Vanessa,' Tamara said.

'I don't know about jealous. But Vanessa had been needling her from the moment she got here. Perhaps you didn't notice it.'

'She needled everybody.'

'That's true. More likely to be murdered than to commit suicide, in fact.'

Tamara did not answer, and after a moment's silence Giles said quietly, 'I don't know what made me say that.'

'Could anyone else have come on board?'

A faint mist was rising from the water; it looked luminous in the glow of the moon, which was nearly full. A murmur of voices came across from the workmen's barge. Nobody on it seemed to have noticed the disturbance. On the muddy patch of shore where the gangplanks rested, a white-robed man squatted beside his glowing brazier, an immobile, timeless watchman. 'Not without him noticing,' Giles said.

'What is he guarding us from?' Tamara asked.

'Assassins.'

Giles called out in the man's language, and the crouched figure stood slowly and turned so that the faint light glinted on his eyes. He answered briefly, and a second question at greater length. 'Nobody came on board tonight,' Giles said.

'You believe him?'

'As far as one can believe a man from a strange culture, speaking a strange language, with strange prejudices and loyalties that I could never hope to comprehend, yes, I believe him. I have not known him lie to me in my four seasons here. He says that nobody except Abdullah the waiter and Hassan the chamber man have come on board this evening.'

'And he's always there?'

'He and his mate take turns, twenty-four hours a day. It's a custom one doesn't interfere with. He sleeps later, sitting up like a log. He'd wake up for a stranger, but somehow sleeps through if anyone he knows passes by.'

'Like a dog?'

Giles said coldly, 'I'd stake my own life on none of them having anything to do with this.'

'I'd almost stake my life on Vanessa not realising they were people at all.'

'Servants would have been furniture to her,' he agreed. He knocked his pipe against the rail, emptying its contents, and took an envelope of tobacco from his pocket to re-fill it. He said, 'It's ridiculous, I know. I spend my life studying dead societies; dead people; and everything about the Egyptian past reminds one of it. Death obsessed them. I must have excavated dozens of graves in my time. You probably have yourself. But now I feel completely thrown. Why do we find a contemporary corpse so shocking?'

'Because it is a shock to see it,' Tamara said calmly.

'I suppose it will be the end of this season's work. It might be the end of the whole dig. It's more difficult every year to get a permit as it is. The Egyptians are increasingly sticky about having foreigners poking around their antiquities. You can't blame them. And until you have seen officialdom at work in this country you have never seen it properly. Don't forget their ancestors invented bureaucracy. They controlled an empire with it for five millennia.'

'Probably worse the further from the centre you are,' Tamara said sympathetically.

'And we are so close to the border. What the Sudanese would say . . .'

'Has nobody else ever died here?'

'Not in my time. And not foreigners. But I took over from old Fred Harper, do you know who I mean?'

'I heard him lecture once.'

'He had a season when the natives were going down like flies. They thought the place was cursed, but it all turned out to be due to some kid's disease. Measles, I think.'

'So what happened?'

'They carried on throughout. It's all in the site notebooks. Five of them died in the end, and of course you couldn't keep the bodies hanging round too long in this climate. They put them in the Roman sarcophagi.'

'On the shore over there?'

'No, this was before the flooding. They'll be fathoms deep by now.'

'Well,' Tamara said, deliberately flippant. 'That means that there are some spare spaces in case we need them. And if the tug isn't mended by tomorrow, my prediction is that we are very likely to.'

10

Timothy Knipe was asleep, as one could easily hear, and nobody else at Qasr Samaan had any personal reason to regret the death of Vanessa Papillon. All the same, the universally self-regarding reaction was noticeable.

How is this going to affect me? was clearly the thought in everybody's head, not least Tamara's own, or as he had admitted, Giles's. For the others, Tamara supposed there might be silver linings to the cloud, if it was cloud and not the sun bursting from behind them. Giles had said that Vanessa needled people. Tamara would have used a far stronger word. Tormented, perhaps.

Janet Macmillan, of course, had walked straight into Vanessa's line of fire by choosing to take the same Egyptian tour. And yet she had chosen it because Vanessa would be there; that had become clear enough – unless she had forgotten Vanessa in following Tim. Did she love Tim so desperately that she wanted to be in his company no matter how painfully? Had she hoped to make him suffer? Had she wanted to spoil Vanessa's enjoyment of her new acquisition? Had she at last done so, in the most drastic of ways?

Tamara was sure of one thing at least. Janet had come to Qasr Samaan, come on this trip, from personal motives, not for any reason that would, or would once, have interested Mr Black.

Tamara had always doubted that Janet was likely to

betray her country or that publicising her discovery would have been a betrayal.

'Just because she comes from Cambridge,' Tamara had said to Mr Black who had been at Oxford. 'Having the Cambridge traitors on the brain is your occupational hazard.'

Mr Black was the sort of man that high-spirited young women tended to address with mild impertinence. It was not flirting. To Tamara, and she always assumed to others like her, he exuded sexlessness, quite apart from the fact that he was a friend and a contemporary of her father. It seemed necessary to choose between subservience and cheek; and the sort of person who became a secret agent was unlikely to be humble. The sort of man who became a spy master was not likely to take cheek amiss.

'Two points,' he had replied. 'Firstly, that treachery from families like Janet's is not unknown. Secondly, that she is a woman scorned.'

'An old-fashioned view,' the young feminist had said. But she thought about it all the same. Women have died and worms have eaten them, and even for love. Women have betrayed, and their countries have reviled them, also for love. Or, in this case, she thought, for altruism.

Tamara had no idea how Janet's equations reached the results she had wished to broadcast. Tamara did not need to know the researcher's progress or process, merely what she had found she could do. In searching for and, she believed, finding a treatment for epilepsy, she had discovered a way of inducing it.

It was to do with the frequencies of subsonic waves, the speed of flashing lights and something known as alpha rhythms or theta waves in the brain. The explanation seemed to involve a good many of the letters in the Greek alphabet, and they were the only part that was not Greek to Tamara. She felt, not for the first time, the old shame of an arts graduate obliged to confess innumeracy.

No scientific education was required to know that it was desirable to discover a method of warding off epileptic attacks that did not bring the side-effects of drug-based treatments. Janet had found a way to provide such a thing. She had been working on a method of enabling a sufferer to alter mechanically the electrical rhythms of the brain. It had started off from a technique in which the patient watched an electrogram of his or her own brainwaves and adjusted them by an act of will alone.

In order to study the elimination of the stimuli that caused epileptic seizures, Janet had been working on a way of causing them. After all, Mr Black explained, weapons defence systems can only be made by someone who knows how to make weapons, and laboratories making antidotes to poisons have to analyse the poisons first.

'Weapons?' Tamara had interrupted.

'Unfortunately,' Mr Black replied, 'the silly girl has discovered a universal method of synchronisation without even realising it.'

Janet had worked out a system to measure the specific amplitude and intensity of brainwave patterns, and the exact arrangement of stimuli that could cause major fits.

A major fit, Mr Black explained, often called grand mal, caused muscular spasms followed by total amnesia about the period during which the fit took place.

A minor fit, petit mal, was known by the boffins (Mr Black's expression and voice were gently disdainful) as sense-specific fits. The body is temporarily paralysed, or the power of sight momentarily disappears, but the sufferer remains conscious. Even a minor fit would incapacitate an enemy.

'An enemy?' Tamara exclaimed.

The technique could keep the human brain from epilepsy. But it could induce epilepsy too. It could do so not only in people known to be susceptible, but in anybody; in, for example, an opposing army.

'It is obvious to anyone who isn't blinded by the intellectual delight of pure research. Janet Macmillan's boss tried to make her see why she couldn't publish.'

'One can sympathise with her,' Tamara said. 'Especially as it sounds most unlikely. It sounds so specific. So individual. How could one use it on a mass of people?'

'It is neither individual nor universal. It would work over short distances only. For instance across fortified borders – over a front line. But if you could knock out, say, every tenth man . . .'

'But if you could cure every epileptic . . .'

'That was what Dr Macmillan said too. You and she ought to get on quite well.'

Tamara and Janet had got on quite well. Two clever, well-educated, successful women, much of an age, from similar backgrounds, they had immediately spoken the same language and identified numerous shared acquaintances, including Tamara's elder sister Alexandra. They had not exactly become friends. Both were too preoccupied by their separate, secret considerations. In other circumstances, they might have done so. But Tamara now accepted that this was a voyage of unrealisable possibilities; friendship with Janet, something more than friendship with Giles Needham, who was quite as attractive a man and quite as worth pursuing as poor Vanessa Papillon had made no secret of thinking. And now both were under suspicion, even if only by Tamara whose function did not include wondering about murder.

It was hard to put the possibility out of her mind down on the sleeping deck, kept awake by snores and the drifting smell, or perhaps its memory or its possibility – Tamara could not tell whether the smell was in her nose or in the air outside the cubicle where Vanessa lay dead in her mess.

There was aural evidence that at least three of the party were asleep. The others were silent, and none were upstairs. The generator had ceased its hum.

Tamara had more than one flashlight and an ample supply of batteries. But she lay still in a darkness relieved only by a faint oblong of lesser blackness. The nightly mist obscured the light of the stars that earlier had been so brilliant.

It isn't anything to do with me, she thought rebelliously, fearing, knowing that fate had chosen her to volunteer as remorselessly as an old-style sergeant major would pick on some unwilling soldier with the cruel phrase.

The bottle she had taken from Vanessa's side was wrapped in some of her underwear. It was in her suitcase. Even by torchlight Tamara could see that the water was a little cloudy. She dipped her finger into the liquid and tasted it, being careful not to swallow, and spitting and wiping her tongue with a paper tissue afterwards.

She could not tell. Was she imagining a bitter flavour? And if not, what good would it do her to know it? The intensive course that she had been put through before going onto Mr Black's staff had not included rapid identifications of poisons, only advice as to how to avoid having any forced upon her.

If anyone had put poison into Vanessa's water there must have been a strong motive for it. With deep reluctance, Tamara realised that there might be some evidence of that motive in Vanessa's belongings.

Tamara groped under her bed for a pair of locally acquired sandals with hard leather soles. They made an audible click as she went along the passage to the toilet cubicles. There, she stepped out of them, and padded barefoot and silently to the door of Vanessa's room. She eased it open. In all the dreadful detail the cabin was as they had left it earlier in the evening. Perhaps everyone had idiotically thought, hoped, that some other hand would put things to rights or could undo disaster.

Assailed by the smell, Tamara pressed one hand over her nose. With the other she aimed the shaft of light around. Somewhere there must be at least the notebook without which a professional journalist would not travel. It was impossible to search without leaving obvious signs that somebody had done so. The image of the mess that she would have to disturb must be imprinted on other memories too. Nor was there time. How long could she plausibly seem to be in the lavatory?

Tamara's toe stubbed against something hard. It was a small tape-recorder. That was it. Of course a woman of the spoken word like Vanessa would dictate, not write, her notes. Tamara scooped it quickly up. No time to hunt for the spares.

It was a relief to get out of the room. The image of that dead face, masked, momentarily highlit by the beam of the flashlight, was a memory that Tamara wished she did not have to store.

She pulled the plug loudly and tapped her way back to her own privacy.

Tamara's earphones fitted into Vanessa's tape-recorder but her batteries did not. Those already in it lasted long enough to make the tape rewind, and to let Tamara hear a description of herself, characteristically acid. Was she a Petra Pan, clinging to an appearance of juvenility? Did she contrive to appear uncontrived? The criticism was irrelevant, untimely, and should be as quickly forgotten as heard; but lying back on her bed, frustrated of more interesting eaves-droppings, Tamara found herself reflecting more on herself than on Vanessa and whoever might have killed her.

But after all, she thought, what does it matter to me? What matters is that I manage to get Janet, and at least one other of the people at Qasr Samaan, safely home.

11

There seemed no reason to delay the scheduled departure in the morning. None of the party would be sorry to leave Vanessa behind – to leave the problems to Giles.

Ann Benson punctually complained that she could not get her belongings into the case that had accommodated them on the way down; it was business – or pleasure – as usual. Giles was dressed in a linen suit, with a striped tie. Tamara wondered whether any of the officials he needed to impress would recognise the message of the narrow blue stripes across the black background. He looked very much the English milord; which might have quite the opposite, nowadays, of the desired effect.

Everybody was to go to Abu Simbel together. Giles Needham would do whatever was necessary about the late Vanessa. The Camisis party would return, one short, to Aswan, and fly from there as planned, to Cairo and on to London.

The tug could not be made to start.

The Nubians had been working on it since dawn. Their energy and excitement was admirable but ineffective. The patriarchal captain remained impassive on the deck, watching his men as they toiled over the engine.

Giles asked him a question and the patriarch threw his hands upwards and looked at the sky. '*Inshallah*,' Giles reported to the waiting Britons. 'As God wills.'

'But that simply is not good enough,' John Benson said.

'You can hardly expect us to wait here in such circumstances.'

'He's doing his best, you must admit,' Ann Benson murmured.

'Where is Max Solomon? It's for him to do something about this. Our contract with Camisis . . .'

Max Solomon was still in his cabin. Hugo Bloom had looked in on him, and said he seemed to be on his third notebook. 'Might as well leave him to get on with it, don't you think?'

'When an artist is inspired, you know what I mean,' Ann Benson began.

'Inspired. Nonsense. It's his job to get us away from here. He must do something,' her brother said.

'About the body, do you mean?' Hugo Bloom asked.

The body; that was really the problem.

All the British people present had enough knowledge of their own country's police procedure, whether from books, or television programmes, or even from experience, to have been sure that they weren't supposed to touch anything in that ghastly chamber until the proper authorities had had the chance to examine it. They had been only too glad to assume that the same rules applied in the furthest reaches of Upper Egypt. Nobody had the least inclination to interfere with the hideous remains.

If it had been possible to fetch help as quickly as the tug could travel, it would have been almost too late, in this climate, for the authorities to see, or those who cleared up after them to cope.

Stuck at Qasr Samaan themselves, marooned, they could hardly leave the body or the mess surrounding it, untouched for even half a day. Something was going to have to be done. Someone was going to have to do it.

John Benson predictably asserted that the native servants should clear up this, as they did other messes.

'I hardly think we can expect that of them,' Hugo Bloom said. 'There must be one of us who has some experience of illness.'

Timothy Knipe was behaving as though the whole thing was nothing to do with him. He talked to Polly about sex while she sorted out potsherds, arranging them as though they were jig-saw pieces.

Ann Benson said, 'I couldn't. I am sorry but I simply couldn't. Hugo, you know that I am not . . .'

'My dear girl. Of course not.'

'We couldn't expect such a thing of you,' Giles Needham said. 'Not of any of you. But something will have to be done if we are stuck here.'

John Benson had stalked away to stand glowering across at the tug, where the work looked increasingly frenzied. Ann went to stand beside him, talking anxiously. The others could hear her protests of self-abnegation. She knew that she should be strong enough to cope with such things. She was ashamed of her own weakness. 'But I simply can't see it, her, again, I'd die. I would really die. Johnny, you do understand why I . . .'

On and on.

Hugo, Janet, Tamara and Giles found themselves like grownups left to make the necessary arrangements while the children went off to sulk, argue or play.

'A sleeping bag,' Tamara said. 'Are there any?'

'Hardly, in this climate.'

'We need a kind of body-bag. Or shroud.'

'There are plenty of sheets. The ancients used winding sheets,' Giles said.

'Several layers, anyway,' Tamara agreed.

'That's the first thing.'

The local servants insisted on doing the cleaning up in the end, which was one small relief. Another was that the excavation equipment included a supply of rubber gloves.

The limbs were mobile. Rigor mortis must have come and gone in the lonely night. When Tamara tried to close the staring eyes they sprang open again in a parody of the live Vanessa's topaz gaze. Hugo Bloom produced a pair of coins and put them archaically on the eyelids. Janet tied up the jaw with a bedouin scarf Vanessa had bought in Luxor. Between them the four survivors wrapped the body in the rough cotton sheets, and then tore more of them into strips to wind around the white bundle. It reminded Tamara of the swaddling of a baby she had once watched on a television anthropology programme.

'I saw a local funeral when we were moored at Esna,' Hugo Bloom said. 'They were carrying the body high in the air, wailing.'

'Is this how it had been wrapped?'

'As far as one could see. It could do with some of the sweet-smelling herbs though.' That was the first reference to the smell.

Tamara wiped her arm across her wet forehead. She said, 'Would some Diorissimo do?'

'It would be too small a drop in this ocean. Anyway, you will need it yourself, later.'

It was amazing what one could do if one had to. Janet seemed dispassionate and business-like. She pulled and tugged at the strips of fabric as though they were ingredients of an experiment. Giles and Hugo too worked like surgeons, subduing easy emotion to the necessary task. Tamara would not allow herself to flinch. With four pairs of hands the work was done not quickly, for it felt like an eternity, but properly, so that it was possible to feel that the oval white package was no more terrible than a closed coffin.

Giles summoned Abdullah and Hassan to help the men carry it out, and after animated, but, on the servants' side, sympathetic conversation, he said, 'They say they will clean up the room. They don't seem to mind.'

The shrouded body was laid on the bed in Giles's own cabin.

'You aren't superstitious about it?' Hugo said.

'Only to the extent that I'll want clean sheets tonight.' And to the extent that he pulled the small curtain across the porthole and spoke in a whisper. 'We had better get cleaned up. And then I'll see how they are getting on with the tug.'

Washed, changed, and sprayed with a good deal of the Diorissimo, Tamara could begin to feel that she might forget the unspeakable smell. She did not expect ever to forget the feeling, the unmitigated sight, of Vanessa's remains. As Giles had remarked the previous evening, any archaeologist lives with the material traces of death. Tamara, more than any archaeologist, she supposed, also had some knowledge of causing it. But she had never wondered before about the purely practical nature of the event. Somebody always had to clear up the messes. She hoped that it would not again be her.

Back in her room she inserted the small batteries she had found in Vanessa's drawer into Vanessa's recorder. She had found three of the tiny tape cassettes too, all of which she had been able to pocket. It would be a long and weary chore to listen to it all, unable to wind fast forward for fear of missing a vital phrase. It was another confirmation of Tamara's preference for the written page. She could read in thirty seconds what it would take ten times as many to hear.

By the time of the midday meal Tamara had managed to play only one side of the tape that had been in the machine, presumably the most recently recorded.

The adjectives Vanessa had dictated as an aide memoire for her own future use would not have enticed her hearers to go to Qasr Samaan. Dusty, hot, bored, imprisoned, uncomfortable and ill fed, her death came at what sounded like a low point in her life. She had decided that Giles was not as attractive as he had seemed on the screen. 'Pompous, boringly obsessed by his petty scholarship and positively rude,' the rich voice murmured into Tamara's ear. 'Not the man for a woman like me. He would do for one of the blue stockings. Hoyland is the one he looks at. I can't be sure whether she has noticed, under that cool, cagey stare of hers. Nuisance that I didn't have time to get more research done on her. There was something fishy about that last-minute change of lecturer. Or on Polly. No, not a nuisance. I would not want anyone else to know that she's here. Not yet. What a scoop. I knew there would be a good story for me here, I just didn't know what it would be. I shall corner her later. I wonder whether she knows what is going on back home. Could she be such a twit that she never thought what would happen if she just took off to Egypt? Wait a minute. She can't have travelled in her own name. That passport never went through a British port. Come to think of it, she probably doesn't even have a passport. How did she get here then?'

The famous voice, thinking aloud for its speaker's ears only, was beautiful. Tamara had never fully understood before that there could be music in spoken words and suddenly, for the first time, and perhaps alone of those at Qasr Samaan, she mourned for Vanessa.

Lunchtime. Hassan seemed to be swinging the hand bell with respectful restraint, and had even muffled the clapper in the presence of death.

There was no hurry to hear more of Vanessa's perceptions. But Tamara was interested that the first had confirmed her own.

At lunch, a meal for which the four people who had undertaken the task of shrouding the corpse felt little enthusiasm, there was still some hope that the party would get away from Qasr Samaan that day.

Subdued attempts to converse broke long silences. It was the most ill-assorted party Tamara could imagine. Echoing her thought, Hugo Bloom remarked that it was probably like this in prison, shut up with other people; he did not need to add, that one would be shut up with people not of one's own choice.

'I wonder what is happening at home,' Ann Benson said.

'One quite misses the bore with his World Service,' her brother admitted.

'A cold and muddy February,' Hugo Bloom said.

'I am missing the English weather. Do you know what I mean?' Ann Benson said. 'I have seen enough of the sun to last me a lifetime. I really wish we had never come here in the first place.'

'Oh come on, Ann. Football riots, the balance of payments, a railway strike – we are well out of it,' Hugo said cheerfully.

'I must admit I would like to know what's going on. For instance, do you think they have found the Princess yet?'

'Sorry, careless of me,' Polly said, picking up her knife from the floor.

'Found who?' Giles asked.

'Princess Mary. Didn't you hear the news?'

'Of course not. The world could come to an end without our knowing about it when we are here. What news?'

Ann Benson seemed to relish telling of the young Princess's abduction.

'I cannot bear the way you all speak as though this young woman matters so much more than anyone else,' John said.

'Because she's over-privileged, you mean?' Tim asked.

'She may be suffering. She's a victim,' Hugo said.

Ann said, 'It seems funny, do you know what I mean, that we're so close to the people who must have done it.'

'What do you mean?' Giles said sharply.

'If the motive was to get food for the Sudanese . . . you said yourself we were very close to the border. Would we have heard the aeroplanes of supplies going over, do you think?'

'Did you say . . .' Polly paused to clear her throat. 'What did you say had happened exactly? Didn't she . . . wasn't there a message or something?'

'That's the point. She's been kidnapped by a group of people who don't want any ransom. They are demanding food for the starving people in the Sudan. Crime in a good cause, you might say,' Tamara said. 'Perhaps the girl even arranged it herself. One would rather admire her if she had.'

'How silly.' Polly flounced to her feet. 'Oh look. Here's the captain coming.'

The patriarch came onto the barge miming apology in every inch of his body. The barge could not, would not be made to start. There could be no question of leaving for Abu Simbel before dusk.

By the middle of the afternoon it was clear that they would not be able to set off then either. Clothes and belongings were taken from their cases again. Those who could, slept. Others moped or read. Tamara asked Polly to show her the excavation's technical equipment.

A lean-to shed made of corrugated iron housed the make-shift laboratories at the stern end of the upper deck. Its metal casing acted as an oven in the tropical sun.

'It really is the black hole of Calcutta,' Tamara gasped.

'I don't know how the photographer stands it. I only come and help him very early in the morning,' Polly said. She pointed out the neatly labelled jars of chemicals. 'Better not touch. There are some things here that you wouldn't be allowed to have around back home.' Hand-drawn skulls and crossbones were stuck to the dangerous substances. Nothing but that warning seemed to protect them.

'For goodness sake, let's get out into the shade,' Tamara said. Under the awning, the breeze made the temperature of the afternoon tolerable. Polly loosened her hair ribbon and pulled at the tendrils that had fallen onto her face, tucking them back to tie out of the way.

'It makes you want to cut it all short,' she complained.

'Why don't you?'

'But who could do it here? Anyway I'd look horrid with short hair.'

Tamara's hair was held back in a pair of combs. Her colouring was much fairer than Polly's, but she seemed less affected by the heat. 'How long have you been out here?' she said.

'Long enough. Since just after Christmas.'

'You joined Giles after the beginning of the season then? I thought he had begun work in November.'

'Yes. It was arranged by a professor at Buriton University. She's a friend of Giles's, so he agreed to do it as a favour.'

'Really? I wonder— '

'A favour to my father actually,' Polly said. 'He's a professor at Buriton himself.'

'I know the Professor of Archaeology at Buriton. Thea Crawford was my tutor when I was doing research at London,' Tamara said. 'Nice place to live, I should think, so pretty in that part of Cornwall.'

'Is that Giles calling me?' Polly stood up.

'I didn't hear anything.'

'I'd better go and see.' Polly was wearing a green dress made in crinkled, patterned cotton that dangled sadly around her ankles. Its limp folds kept catching on the furniture, and there were little triangular tears in the fabric. She twitched her hips so that the material swirled behind her as she clattered down the stairs.

Tamara pulled her chair out into the sunshine and lay back in it, her eyes closed. She felt sorry for Polly; but did she have to feel responsible for her too?

What a fool the girl was, silly and self-willed, influenced, probably, by the catch phrase that journalists used of her ever since an early, public tantrum; 'What Polly wants, Polly gets.' It was a joke at first, printed when Polly was a child, round, rosy and self-confident, very appealing. The adjectives changed as she grew older; determined, strong-minded, bossy, a person who knew her own mind.

Those were, perhaps, other words for irresponsibility. Why should anyone protect the girl from the consequences of her own stupidity? And, indeed, it would not have been possible to do so, with Vanessa on the trail of a story that no journalist could leave untold. Polly must have known that Vanessa would tell the world where she had found the Princess Mary.

'Deep in thought, I see,' Ann Benson said. 'Oh, I am sorry. I startled you, didn't I?'

'I am afraid I was half-asleep.'

'I am going to sleep too. I just came up to fetch my reading glasses, I think I must have left them here. John always says that I scatter my belongings like autumn leaves. He can't bear it. Oh yes, here they are. I see you have your cassette player. What are you listening to?'

'It's a Marvin Gaye tape,' Tamara said, certain that it would not be the kind of sound Ann Benson would ask to borrow.

'Oh, that's your modern music. John says he won't dignify it with the name. Noise, he says, not music. But I always say it's in the ear of the beholder, if you know what I mean.'

Tamara could almost behold the face from which the voice in her ear had come, so vivid was it in her mind as she listened.

'Perhaps I'll try Hugo Bloom. He's quite attractive in a wiry kind of way. He looks capable of most things. He might be interesting. I wonder what he does at the

Bensons' famous Fernley. I asked him whether he knew anything about that place next door that Olly once told me was a Safe House. He looked . . . what? Dangerous. Tough. I quite fancy him, and Tim's becoming a bore. Silly Polly has no idea of the fuss there is about her back home. She came in a friend's place and left a letter for the family to say she had gone. She did not know they never got it. I suppose the friend took advantage of the opportunity to do some altruistic extortion. I am going to have some fun with this.'

So Vanessa had not only recognised Polly but had let her know it. Polly cannot have been left in much doubt as to the use that she would make of the information. Would she have minded very much? And if she minded, how far would she have gone to do something about it? The motive, the opportunity, the means; murder would have been easy for any of them, and tempting to several, Tamara thought gloomily.

All the more reason to get the girl safely home. The mind boggled at the idea of a British princess incarcerated in an Egyptian or even a Sudanese gaol awaiting trial on a murder charge.

The cassette had ended, but the earpieces muffled any sounds from the outside. Tamara had every intention of listening to more of Vanessa's aides memoires. She would just close her eyes for a tiny moment. Dreamlessly, she slept.

Shortly before dusk, when the lowering, reddening sun lay almost behind the rocky hills to the west, four of the workmen, wearing white galabiehs, brought Vanessa's body upstairs, and lowered it down into a small dinghy. One man ferried it across to a party of his friends waiting on the lake-shore. He then returned to fetch two boats full of the Europeans.

The Nubians were intoning what sounded like a respectful dirge.

'Are they Christians?' John Benson asked sharply.

'Several of them wear crucifixes,' Hugo said.

Whether Christian or Muslim, all seemed willing to attend the unconventional cortège, standing at a little distance, with a dignity that came less naturally to Vanessa's erstwhile companions, though all of them except Max Solomon were there.

Max was asleep across his bed, on top of, by now, five full notebooks. There had been a general, undiscussed agreement not to wake or interrupt him. Indeed, the respect for his revived muse was a far more strong and universal emotion among the Europeans than for the ceremony that they were now attending.

It was all too bizarre for the proper emotions. Only Polly cried, a childish sobbing that grated on adult nerves.

John Benson, who alone of the men present knew the words of the burial service, intoned in a High Church sing-song that seemed not imposing but absurd. When he reached the stage of dropping earth on a coffin he paused, suddenly at a loss; for the body was not below his feet in ashes and dust.

After an awkward pause the workmen came forward, and in unison swung forward to lift the white bundle into the stone cist where once a Roman soldier, hardly less distant from his home, had left his bones. The flat slab that had been its cover was heaved up to block the opening.

By now darkness had fallen, and as usual the wind had subsided. Nothing was to be heard but the slapping of the wavelets against the shore. It was not romantic but frightening and disorientating to be standing in as formal clothes as each person could muster, separated by two hundred yards of water from the barges moored at Qasr Samaan, in a threatening vastness of empty desert.

Everyone waited in an awkward silence. After a while Giles Needham said, 'If the authorities let her remain here I'll get Mahmoud to carve her name on it. He's a wonderful stone mason.'

'She was called Vera Pritchard,' Tamara said.

'How do you know?' Ann Benson said.

'Max mentioned it. His son Jonty worked with her. Naturally she didn't want people to know. Vanessa Papillon, the butterfly, suited her better.'

Timothy Knipe began to laugh. 'Bogus to the very last. They'll call the wrong name for her on Judgement Day.' He giggled and snorted until Janet Macmillan shook him sharply and said, 'Shut up, damn you. Shut up.'

Disconsolate, the small group of marooned travellers returned for another night in the immobile barge.

12

Tamara Hoyland as Hercule Poirot. She could not help feeling that there had been a mistake in the casting.

Stir it a bit, she thought, and said, 'It reminds me of *Death on the Nile*.' Except, she did not say aloud, that the dramatis personae looked so very much less glamorous than those in the film. Without Vanessa to lend elegance, those present could more plausibly have been acting in a drama of modern realism. Only Giles and Hugo had properly acclimatised to the sun and were smoothly brown; Polly's skin was speckled with pale patches grown over sunburn and insect bites.

Janet Macmillan was polka-dotted with freckles. The thick bones of her large face seemed to jut under the skin as though she had lost weight very quickly. She had the kind of head that might have been sculpted in stone, with angular planes and what Tamara thought would once have been called a chiselled nose. Beside her Tamara felt puny. She wondered how their skeletons would compare.

Ann Benson's hands and face had erupted in a rash, while John was pinkly sunburnt. Exposure neither tanned nor burnt Tim Knipe who, always pale, hardly looked more so at this moment, and would have been welcomed on the set of an escapist film. He still contrived to look both piratical and poetical.

Max Solomon, of course, was not with the rest of the party. He had not joined them for any meal since Vanessa's death, though he seemed to have nibbled something from the trays of food his Nubian steward carried down. The servants had decided that he was a wise and possibly a holy man, Giles said.

Tamara went on, 'If this were Agatha Christie, Vanessa would have been murdered.'

'By Tim,' Janet said.

'You don't expect me to have read that muck,' Tim said. He was on his third glass of brandy and two full ashtrays were on the table in front of him. The others had left a little space on either side as they all sat around the long table so that Tim could sprawl and stretch, or simply rest his shaggy head on his folded arms in front of him. He was at once restless and dazed. But then everybody seemed to be not changed, but more noticeably what they normally were, watchful like Hugo Bloom or Polly (though her attention was focused on Giles alone) or abstracted, like Janet, or babbling, like Ann Benson.

'It made such a wonderful film,' she said, bravely ignoring a contemptuous glance from her brother. 'The scenery!'

'In the story, as far as I recall,' Tamara said, 'two people had conspired together to murder someone who was the wife of one and the former friend of the other.'

'The man had married the wrong woman, don't you remember?' Ann Benson said. 'She'd fallen for her best friend's young man. Stolen him really.'

Her brother said, 'I cannot bear people who speak of people as though they were property.'

'Haven't you all read it, or seen the film at least?' Ann Benson asked. 'It was what made me want to come. Well, not this so much, but the river steamer. It looked so lovely. They showed it last winter, it was cold outside and the kitchen roof was leaking, and then that lovely sight . . . blue water and sky and everyone wearing thin clothes with sun hats, it looked like Heaven. Don't you remember, John? You must do. He pretends not to be watching,' she confided to the assembled company. 'He always sits there, straight in front of the set with a book on his lap, and says he doesn't hear a thing. But I see him looking at the screen really. Come on, John, admit it.' Her face was flushed, perhaps with the excitement of liberty, for her brother looked at her as though she had never spoken to him so openly before. 'And then there was the temple. The one where the baddy pushed a rock down to try to kill someone. Or was that a different film? I forget. But it was all hot and dusty and windy and sort of frightening, like where you and Mr Bloom were today, Janet, when you went off together and I was up above you on the hill and I thought how easily I could just roll one of those boulders down . . .'

'Perhaps it was a mistake to give her brandy,' Giles muttered to Tamara.

'You were talking about science. You're so clever to be a scientist. I couldn't understand a word you said, all those letters and numbers. But you wrote them all down, didn't you, Mr Bloom? I watched you. In your notebook. And then Janet tried to take it off you and you wouldn't let her. But we know what that sort of scuffle leads to, don't we?' She giggled. If she had known the phrase she would have said 'nudge nudge wink wink', and Janet Macmillan blushed as though she had.

'Have another drink and shut up,' Timothy Knipe growled. Ann Benson gasped, giggled some more and held out her glass.

'Not for my sister, thank you,' John Benson said.

'Not? Perhaps I am just the least little bit squiffy,' she admitted. 'It was seeing it . . . her . . . Vanessa. So unexpected. I mean, I have seen people in dreadful states before, dead even, but not like that. Not suddenly like that. And when it's in a film it doesn't look so horrible somehow. Or you can just close your eyes, or think about something else.

I mean, the murder is just a part of the fun, like a game or something. Not a real person, vomiting and smelling so horrible and then being . . . I'm going to be sick myself.' She lurched away from the table and they heard her clattering down the stairs and along the passage.

'I should apologise for my sister. She isn't herself. That's what I can't bear about modern entertainment like television. It allows the deluded viewer to suppose that horrors can always be sanitised.'

'But this is a rather different event in any case,' Tamara said. 'I mean, Vanessa was not actually murdered, was she?'

Giles Needham looked at her very sharply, and then said, 'What would we do if she had been?'

'Ask the usual questions, I suppose. How, when, where, why – and, of course, who. Whom is all we do know.'

'How,' Giles said, holding up his first finger. 'How did she die?'

'Luckily the answer is obvious enough to make proceeding with the other questions either unnecessary or undesirable,' John Benson said. He pushed his chair sharply backwards, its metal legs screeching against the deck. 'I see no point in this distasteful conversation. I shall retire to bed.' He followed his sister down the stairs. Tim Knipe was already asleep and snoring at the table, and Polly had slid onto the floor, where she reclined at Giles Needham's feet, her cheek against his knee. Her mouth had fallen unbecomingly open, and she was dribbling slightly.

'How, then?' Hugo Bloom said, looking from Giles to Tamara and back. 'I at least am interested.'

'Food poisoning, surely,' Giles Needham said. He shifted Polly's head without waking her, to reach his pipe from his pocket. The match flame, sucked in and out through the tobacco, fitfully illuminated his down-turned face. The single hanging, unshaded bulb that lit the whole long living deck, threw an ugly and inadequate light on the people who remained up there. By this time on the previous two evenings everybody had already been in bed.

There was something indefinably sinister about sitting in this comfortless enclosure, its chill emphasised by the few attempts that had been made since the excavation season began to make it less unhomely. A large calendar showing a carthorse in a snow-covered field, and some picture postcards of the Alps, were tacked onto the wall. A striped durry covered a small fraction of the floorboards.

Tamara shivered and pulled her cardigan more closely around herself.

'It does get cold at night,' Giles Needham said.

'You feel it if you aren't well,' Hugo said.

'Yes, I have had a sort of tummy upset myself,' Tamara said.

'Better now?'

'Yes thanks, the worst is over.'

'Not for Vanessa.'

'Hers was something much more serious.'

'Brought on by what, I wonder,' Giles said. 'It would be just as well to know. If she had an allergy that's one thing, very dreadful, but nobody else will be at risk. But if she ate something that one of the others might try . . .'

Hugo said, 'You raise a very terrifying prospect. The angel of death stalking through our little party.'

'That is assuming that she didn't take it on purpose,' Giles said.

'Suicide,' Hugo murmured. His fleshy, intelligent face was thoughtful, almost, Tamara thought, wary. She said:

'Not necessarily. She could have thought she was simply treating herself. She travelled with a whole pharmacopoeia, after all.'

'Self-administered,' Giles said. He sounded relieved.

'Let's hope so,' Hugo Bloom said.

'After all,' Tamara said, 'how else? I mean, simply for the sake of argument, could any one of us have given her medicine that might have harmed her? Who had the chance?'

'We all had the chance,' Giles said gloomily. 'Do you two have to produce these nightmarish ideas? Next thing, you'll be saying there's a murderer among us.'

'Murderer!' Polly looked like a child awaking from a nightmare. She knelt up beside Giles, absent-mindedly wiping her chin with the back of her hand.

'No, of course there's no murderer. You were dreaming. I wish you'd go to bed, Polly,' Giles told her.

'I will. I'm on my way.' She moved lazily slowly round the room picking up the belongings she had spent the day scattering round it. A scarf, a sandal, a notebook, a comb and a tube of face cream. 'I can't think why I stayed up so late anyway. Not quite the most scintillating evening of one's whole life.'

Tossing her head she went down the stairs. Hugo sketched a bow as she passed, and then followed after her. He knows, Tamara thought, and so must Giles. She said:

'How does Polly come to be here in the middle of term?'

'It is part of her practical experience.'

'Much more exciting than mine ever was at Edinburgh,' Tamara said. 'I was always bottom up in muddy ditches at road-widening schemes.'

'I agreed to take her as a favour to Thea Crawford.'

The academic world, as Tamara knew very well herself, was criss-crossed with networks of mutual obligation between adults collecting debts on behalf of their children. Queen's Counsels, deans of teaching hospitals, heads of colleges and film producers would find themselves importuned on behalf of some don's daughter. But not, Tamara thought, on behalf of Polly.

Tamara stared hard at Giles, who gave all the signs of being a deeply embarrassed man. Clearing his throat he said:

'Actually I was wondering . . .'

'How much to admit?'

'No, no, absolutely not, just whether you might give Polly a lift back home. Now that there will be a spare place, without Vanessa, that's to say.'

'There will be questions asked, you know. No getting away from it.'

Giles groaned. He ran his hands through his hair. He got up, and sat down again, and clenched and stretched his fingers.

'Oh, God,' he muttered. 'I suppose they all know.'

'I doubt it. They haven't said anything. And most of them have other things to think about.'

'Vanessa knew.'

'She was going to get a scoop, presumably.'

'She tried to con Polly into talking frankly. Said she'd keep it to herself if there was a good reason. That's a laugh. Good reason!'

'Why don't you tell me about it?' Tamara invited him.

The circumstances were encouraging for confidences. The night was chilly but clear, so that they sat in moon and starlight, listening to the agreeable lapping of the water against the barge, and the background crackle of the watchman's fire. It was just the right place for fairy tales. And Giles's story used fairy-tale ingredients; or perhaps, Tamara thought, those of the modern version of the fairy tale, which must be the gossip column.

Giles Needham was embarrassed by the episode from its very start. 'Dances are really not in my line, but if your own supporters' club lays on a fund-raiser . . .' He had not felt able to stay away, however alien to his personality and his commitment he felt a ballroom to be. 'Why they can't simply hand over the money instead of having to dress up like Christmas trees and over-eat and be deafened . . .'

One of the grandest London houses; royalty in the person of Princess Mary to add lustre; jewellery to dazzle, clothes to crush. Giles had felt both dazzled and crushed himself. He was out of place and ill at ease and least of all at ease with the Princess herself who, in compliment to the cause for which the event was raising money, wore a dress reminiscent of a pharaoh's mummy case, and had her eyes outlined in kohl. The room was decorated with swathes of gold and bronze, touched in turquoise. He likened it to being inside a cigarette advertisement, luxurious, unnecessary and in slightly bad taste. There were television cameras and gossip columnists and a whole page of pictures in *Jennifer's Diary*, Tamara recalled, but did not mention it because Giles would despise her for reading a meretricious rag.

'They had made it all so personal. You know, concentrating on me, myself, not my work at all. I had to dance with her.' His tone betrayed the irritation he had felt at the time, forced to shuffle publicly around a dance floor, clutching so public a partner. 'And then . . .'

'She fell for you?'

Polly had insisted on dancing with Giles most of the night. He was not allowed to leave before she did and she would not leave so long as he was there. 'And after that, she kept inviting me to things.' Polly had asked him to parties, shoots and to stay. Giles had resisted the palatial lures. She attended his lectures, causing inconvenience to the learned societies that had invited him, since wherever Polly went, so did sniffers and searchers.

As far as a man can deter a girl and a commoner can deter royalty, Giles had tried to deter Polly. 'Look, I am twelve years older than she is, I am completely uninterested in social life, she is completely uninterested in academic research.'

But Polly had fallen for the glamorous idea implied by those deceptive television programmes. She had seen herself pushing barrows, heaving shovels, even learning to balance a basket of soil on her head like the native workmen. She could see herself standing in a trench with the sun behind her, trowel in hand, helping the buried past to emerge. She would wear loose cotton trousers and a wide-brimmed hat. Her hands would grow hard and capable, her skin be gilded by the sun. 'Today,' she would telegraph to the leaders of the world, 'today I have gazed upon the face of . . .' Whose face? It did not matter. Some lost hero, another Agamemnon or Tutankhamun, who, buried for millennia, would be brought to light by Polly and by Giles Needham.

Polly had worked out her scheme for getting to Qasr Samaan.

'I had this arrangement to take on a girl to oblige Thea Crawford. Someone whose father is a professor at Buriton. Undergraduate, reading history at Oxford, plenty of digging experience. We met in London and she seemed okay. She was going to take charge of the finds register, help Barry with the photography. Paula Crosse, she's called. I even met her father, terribly Blimpish bloke, but he approved of me, I approved of her, fixed up for her to turn up after Christmas. And what happens?'

Tamara could easily guess. Travelling on Paula Crosse's passport, Polly had turned up.

'They were at school together, you see,' Giles explained. 'Polly was spending the New Year with the Crosses, and the two girls did some childish substitution trick that diddled the detectives for a while. She got clean away. Left a note of course; they'll know they don't have to worry about her, but she didn't tell them exactly where she was going and she says that Paula would never admit she knew either. So here she is.'

Giles's first reaction had been to send her straight back. 'Quite apart from the scandal – I mean, I wouldn't ever live it down. Can you see any university taking me seriously again?

And she is no use here. She's bored already and the routine chores are beyond her. She must be bored with me too by now. I'm a dull dog, only interested in the dusty past.'

'So all the drama back home is a nasty surprise for you both,' Tamara said.

Obviously Paula Crosse had failed to deliver the letter that Polly left, and had taken the opportunity to try extortion for a good cause. 'I suppose that by the time Polly gets home safe and sound the food and clothes will have been delivered to the Sudan or wherever they specified,' Giles said.

Tamara very much doubted that the government would have delivered such a ransom even for a more important public figure than Polly. But the cause was good.

'Quite a neat trick, actually,' Tamara said.

Giles was in no mood to admire a contemporary Robin Hood. He sat with his head sunk into his hands.

'The problem is insoluble,' he groaned.

'Not really. Well, it may be for Polly, but that will serve her right. If I get her back with my lot, you will be here for months after that. By the time you are home it will all have blown over.'

'How could it?'

'Easily, if nobody knows where she has been.'

'But what will Polly say?'

'So long as she doesn't say she was at Qasr Samaan,' Tamara said, 'I don't think you need care what she says. Unless, that is, you do care what happens to her.'

'She may have a hard time,' Giles said.

'She won't if everyone thinks that it is the great romance of the century.'

The expression on Giles's face was answer enough. His unusual handsomeness belied his nature, Tamara thought; he was a monomaniac scholar, uninterested in anything that did not have a bearing on his work. He's probably bored by the way women react to him, if he has even noticed it before.

It would have been hard not to realise what Polly was up to; but more subtle allurements were probably quite outside his range of awareness. What a waste.

What Polly wants, Polly gets, Tamara thought. The girl had been watched with the acute attention paid to some rare breed of bird. Binoculars and cameras were trained on her as on more natural phenomena, and as they were on those of her relations whose doings were of more justifiable interest. It was as though she existed as fodder for the insatiable appetite of the various news media.

No amount of formality or dissimulation had hidden her essentially implacable nature, even though nurture had provided so unusual a set of values and certainties. The assumption of the public gaze was bred in the bone. She knew, without any twinge of doubt, that she was interesting, that other people were pleased and flattered by her attention, that what she really wanted she could have.

Was Giles Needham still what she wanted? It could not be wondered at if he was. Handsome, clever, with that aura of glamour that had nothing to do with his words or actions, but that had come over so clearly on his television series, he would be Prince Charming even to a girl who didn't need a prince. But he had no sense of what mattered to girls like Polly, nor, probably, that she mattered. It was bad luck on a princess to have fallen for one of the few men who seemed indifferent to her status; indeed, more than indifferent – inimical.

'Anyone who married Polly would have lots of money for his own work,' Tamara suggested.

'But hard earned. Can you see me in that role?' Giles had not been offended by the remark, or even surprised. Had Polly proposed to him as had Queen Victoria to her true love? But Prince Albert's whole upbringing had been designed to make him a suitable consort. It would be hard to imagine a less amenable one than Giles Needham.

13

Tamara forced herself to listen to most of the remaining cassettes before going to bed. To hear every word would have been unbearable. Vanessa's verbosity was unexpected, considering how sharp and apt she had been professionally. Several times Tamara wound the tape on quickly and listened to sample snatches to find out whether the adjectival accounts of sightseeing, or the memos about future work, were interspersed with useful remarks about her travelling companions.

Vanessa had done, or had ordered to be done for her, a quick search of files on everybody on the Camisis list of fellow passengers. Her sources were probably no superior to those available to Tamara but she had had more time to consult them, and had discovered enough to produce, if she had wanted to, a snappy, catty profile of everybody there except Tamara herself. And as the voyage up the Nile had progressed she had added to her information. By the time the party reached Aswan, each member of the party would have had good grounds for being pleased that Vanessa was no longer being able to broadcast it.

She had lost interest in Timothy very early on. He disappointed her in bed and bored her in conversation. But she had enjoyed teasing or tormenting Janet. 'If looks could kill! Miss Clever Clogs would strike me dead at her feet. I had better make sure not to go near the edge of a precipice with her anywhere near me.' The voice was not that of a woman who genuinely feared an attack. But had she spoken more truthfully than she knew herself?

Whatever would Mr Black say if his precious inventor got incarcerated in a country that would give good money, or perhaps free pardons, to someone who provided such a weapon? A rapid series of possibilities flashed through Tamara's film-trained imagination. Arabs decimating Israelis with a secret death-ray; turning it on each other, on the arrogant West, on . . . enough. For the first time, Tamara could fully understand why she had been assigned the responsibility of getting Janet safely back home. I hope they lock her up, she thought; or no, I suppose I don't. Unless she really did poison Vanessa. It might be a good justification for keeping her out of circulation.

Now was not the time for ethical uncertainty about a secret-bearer's right to liberty. In the limbo that Qasr Samaan had become, it seemed necessary to exert a strict discipline over her thoughts.

Back to Vanessa.

Ironically, it was only because Janet was watching that Vanessa continued to treat Tim as her lover. If Janet had not been there trying to spoil things for Vanessa and Timothy, there would have been nothing left to spoil by the time they got back to London. Vanessa had not been philosophical about her disappointment, and on the second tape a quarrel was recorded. Vanessa sounded so unlike the person she liked the world to see, that it must have been by mistake that she left the tape turning. Tim had come into the room just as Vanessa was reminding herself where she had seen John Benson before.

'It suddenly occurs to me that I saw him at Plinlimmons. It was the sale when Olly wanted to buy that dreadful sentimental pastel of kids around a maypole. The Shadwells were setting up as art lovers, and they bid idiotic figures for some of those oily looking pictures of sailing boats and sunsets. Olly said they were just right for the Shadwells. John Benson was at the back of the sale room looking as pleased as if he had painted them himself. And I asked Olly, how could anyone be sure whether pictures like that were by Park, or Forbes, or whatever the signature was, and he said that there'd be good money in forging second-rate art because not enough care was taken in authenticating it and that's why he was always so careful about provenance. I wouldn't be a bit surprised if John Benson forges the pictures he deals in.'

Vanessa had made more than one barbed remark about painting and art dealing during the course of the voyage. She must have been shooting blind but her instinct for a target was highly developed. Had she hit the bull's-eye?

It was at that point that the tape recorded Tim's coming into Vanessa's room. Their conversation seemed to be the continuation of one already started, a series of accusations and complaints. It ended with Vanessa warning Tim that their association would be over as soon as they reached London. He could get his stuff out of her apartment. 'But not the things I've paid for. They stay behind.' She listed them in mercenary recollection of what must originally have seemed like generosity. She had lavished consumer durables on Timothy Knipe, from silver fountain pens to a soft-topped car.

'But where shall I go?' he had asked, and later on he had insisted that he still adored her and pleaded with her to start again. He had thought they were on their honeymoon. 'You didn't think I'd spend my life with a loser like you?' she had asked. 'Janet can have you back. You'll do fine for her.'

Tamara pressed the fast forward button. She was not a detective, to eavesdrop on personal grief. In fact she was disgusted by her self-imposed work.

Tamara had long since cast off the inhibitions of a good upbringing. She was prepared to tell lies, to overhear other people's conversations and read their private writings; she had learnt to be devious and cunning. She had used her body as a weapon and as a persuader. She had screwed – one could hardly call it making love – a man whose death she later brought about. She had stolen, cheated and deceived. She would have argued that the ends validated the means she had been forced to use. But there were occasions when the means were more than she could find the heart to undertake and when the end less than justified them.

'I am not a detective,' she muttered. All she must do was complete the assignment that Mr Black had set her, as well as the one that he would have set if he had known of it. And to get Janet and Polly safely home she did not need to know the distasteful details of Vanessa's bitchiness; or which of them, if either, had put a stop to it.

Another morning. Another awakening under a glaring sky to the sound of imprecations. The tug had not been mended yet.

'This is getting ridiculous,' Timothy Knipe announced. 'You seem to want to keep us here for ever.'

Giles Needham bunched his fists and stepped abruptly towards Timothy, who cowered back. Giles halted, and breathed in and out twice, nostrils flared. He said, 'Can you possibly imagine that I am stopping you leaving? I long for you to go.'

Pat on its cue came the sound of shouts from the men on the island. A ship had been sighted in the distance and no shipwrecked mariners ever greeted a sail with more fervour than the well-fed and comfortably housed members of what had been a party of pleasure.

The view was obscured today by a hot haze. Giles said that the khamsin that he had been expecting for several days looked as though it was upon them.

'They were talking about it when we were in Aswan, but then nothing came of it,' Tamara said.

'I don't think we shall escape this time,' Giles said.

'At least we shall be away from here,' Ann Benson said.

Giles was not so sure. 'If that's the steamer from Aswan to Wadi Halfa there is no guarantee that it will stop. Anyway, it's going in the wrong direction.' Wadi Halfa was to the south, on the border with the Sudan. 'It is what you might call a nowheresville,' he said.

'What happens there?' Hugo asked.

'Nothing. There is a non-functioning fish-processing plant, that's all. And a bad road southwards.'

'So what are all those people doing?'

'Some are Sudanese traders bringing goods back from Egypt. There are a few Europeans driving from Alexandria down through Africa. I can see a couple of blonde women on the deck.'

'Could one telephone from Wadi Halfa?' Tamara said.

'If the phones work. They don't usually.'

The ship was a small paddle steamer, onto whose side a barge like their own was tied, and behind which trailed a string of small, bobbing dinghies. The deck of both the steamer and the barge was crammed with people in what looked like standing room only.

The passengers waved and so did the islanders. Their sign language was mutually incomprehensible. Ann Benson rushed down to fetch a sheet and stood waving her white flag. One of the deck cargo found a similar swathe of fabric and waved it back. They shouted. The other shouted.

'Not waving but drowning,' Timothy Knipe said.

Giles spoke urgently to the captain of his own barge. Before the steamer had drawn level with Qasr Samaan, two of the marooned workmen had reached it in the expedition's dinghy, and stood precariously rocking in the disturbed water as they called up to the captain. Gestures and shouts conveyed urgent appeals. But the steamer did not slow down, and just as it was passing out of sight southwards behind the island, one of the messengers was pulled aboard. The other cast off the dinghy, which tossed violently in the steamer's wake until he was able to row it back to base.

Giles tried to cheer his guests up. At least somebody would soon know of their plight.

'Surely there is some alternative. I mean, one could walk along the shore if it came to it,' Timothy Knipe said.

'Where to?' said Giles.

'It's your job to know that.'

'I do know. There is nowhere that you could reach on that terrain in this climate.'

'I am going to have a look at the tug myself,' Hugo said. They watched him cross the two gangplanks, his step jaunty.

'Does he know anything about engines?' Giles said.

'Not that I know of,' Ann Benson told him, but Janet said:

'I wouldn't put it past him. He seems to know an awful lot about an awful lot of things.'

'Why didn't he say so before then?' Timothy muttered. 'He is probably just showing off.'

'I suppose he can't do any harm,' Giles said. He lit his pipe slowly, lowering his eyelids against the puffs of smoke.

'How you can, when it's so hot already,' Polly said fretfully. She waved her hand up and down in front of her face. 'It smells horrid. I would rather you didn't smoke.'

Giles's reply was oblique. 'We are all going to find it hard to keep calm if there's a proper khamsin. Makes one irritable.'

Polly looked surprised, as though even now she expected others to do as she bade them.

'How long, oh Lord, how long?' Tim said.

Giles said, 'I am hoping that the other members of my party will have guessed what has happened and will hire another transport at Abu Simbel. But if they don't turn up today I intend to row to Qasr Ibrim.'

'Where is that? And why wait for tomorrow if it's accessible at all?' Tim demanded.

'Qasr Ibrim is about thirty miles north of us. It is where the American expedition is at work. I spent a season there myself when I was a student. But it will take hours to get there. All day at least. Rowing on Lake Nasser is slow work. And it might not help if I do. Like us, they don't normally have transport available, their tug comes from Abu Simbel at pre-arranged dates, as ours does. I don't want to leave you all here, and be marooned on another island instead myself.'

'Send the men, then. Surely Abdullah could row thirty miles? Or one of the others?'

'Perhaps you would like to come with me?' Giles said.

'I!' Timothy Knipe's jutting beard, modelled on a pirate's, his bright blue eyes, made him look illogically nautical.

'Tim couldn't row three miles, let alone thirty.' Janet was normally so silent that everybody was surprised to hear her speak. Her pale eyes glanced at her former lover. She said, 'He isn't as butch as he looks.'

Timothy Knipe clenched his fists. Giles half-rose. But then Timothy sighed, and smiled with a charm that made two women's passion for him less incomprehensible.

'Janet is right as usual,' he agreed. 'Never known her wrong as a matter of fact. Gets it right every time, this girl does. Private life, work, you name it she hits the spot. Look at her latest project.'

'Shut up, Tim.' Janet seemed to enjoy public praise from Timothy no more than she had enjoyed his public slavering over Vanessa.

'I am going to rout out John,' Ann Benson said. 'He's usually the first up.' It was true that John Benson normally appeared before anyone else for meals, about which he then aired his grievances. No Oxford marmalade, no milk, eggs fried in some unfamiliar native oil – he was preparing a list of complaints for Mr Osmond of Camisis Tours, to which would be appended the fact that Max Solomon had not taken them sufficiently to heart.

As Tamara was pouring herself more coffee, not because she wanted it but because it would occupy a little portion of what was evidently going to be another day of useless waiting, Max Solomon himself appeared, politely wished everyone present a good morning and helped himself to a large plateful of tinned peaches.

He looked around with a kind of innocent curiosity. His face was pale. It had been three days since he had come up into the sun. He also looked changed in some less precise way. He had seemed before a withdrawn, perhaps shy man, who pushed himself against the grain to be friendly and chatty. Tamara had found him kind, almost, at least to her, fatherly, but had sensed all the time that there was an effort going on whereby he controlled what might be an unguarded expression of sorrow, perhaps, or anxiety, of some powerful emotion quite unsuited to the circumstances of relaxed tourism. It had created a barrier that kept all but the most crass members of the party at bay. If his veneer were to crack, something violent and unmanageable might destructively erupt.

And yet, Tamara thought, I am not usually sensitive to such intangibles. Qasr Samaan was affecting her too, but under her usefully expressionless face it was less apparent than in Max Solomon. He seemed in a way washed clean, as though some psychic storm had blown over him, and passed on leaving calm behind.

A little bustle of welcome greeted his appearance. He smiled around and ate with relish, and when Ann Benson came rushing up the stairs he seemed to be prepared to cope as a courier should.

'He's not there. John. He's missing,' she gasped. Her sun-reddened face was blotched and sweaty and her hair was coming down. She provoked, as she always did, a mixture of irritation and pity. 'Where can he possibly be? I can't find him.'

'Are you your brother's keeper?' Timothy Knipe said.

'I did not notice him going on shore,' said Giles. 'Don't you think he is probably in the bathroom?'

'He isn't there. I can't think what has happened to him.'

Unease rippled through the company. Vanessa's death had horrified people less than might have been expected, the idea of it happening in this strange and isolated place neutralised by the pure disgust of it. It had happened, it was over, now the problem was simply the mechanics.

But Ann Benson's terror, irrational and hysterical as it was, produced a reaction in the others that should have been there before; fear that was almost literally panic, contagious and caused by an unseen influence.

By tacit agreement, John Benson was searched for. The door of each room was opened: the photography shed, the toilet cubicles, even the spaces behind the finds boxes and crates of mineral water.

'I am sure he has just gone for a walk before it gets too hot,' Tamara said.

Giles had been speaking to the servants. None of them had seen John Benson. He said, 'We might just go and find him. He can't have gone far, after all.'

They straggled down the gangplank onto the island. Casually they looked behind the blocks of white stone, once part of the church, that lay on the barren ground. Giles, trying not to look like a man who was looking for anything in particular, twitched aside the corners of tarpaulins, and made sure to scan each trench. Ann Benson stumbled ahead, calling her brother's name. Tamara and Timothy Knipe made their way to the little peak of the rock. The water to the south, where it was deeper, was being forced and broken against the land by an increasing wind. On the far shore the closed niche in which Vanessa Papillon's body lay was a reminder of mortality.

The searchers met by the rock known as the bathing place. None of the visitors had dared to risk going in the water, despite Giles's reassurances. But a hat was on the ground, caught by its brim in a crevice of the stone. It was a panama with a band striped in the colours of John Benson's college. His name was written inside on the hatter's label. But of John Benson himself, there was no sign.

14

Now the real nightmare began.

Silence, chatter, tears, screams, questions, exclamations; all the ways were practised in which human beings can demonstrate their distress, anxiety, bafflement and impatience.

From mystification to grief, from irritation to remorse. One could make a graph, Tamara thought, showing the inevitable, invariable pattern of reaction to any disastrous discovery; in this case, to John Benson's disappearance. The indigenous workmen and servants were more dignified, being more disinterested. They helped to search and search again. They looked everywhere that it was conceivably possible for a man to be, alive or dead. Once it seemed undeniable that John Benson was dead, they offered sympathy and withdrew to their own occupations.

There could be no possible explanation for John's disappearance, but that he had somehow drowned in the deep waters of Lake Nasser, and that his body had been carried away where no searcher could find it. Several sweeps around the island in the rowing boat failed to result in any trace of the missing man. The roughened water was clouded by stirred-up sediment. In other circumstances it was easy to see through it to the floor; to see anything that lay on it, in fact.

Whether John had intended to bathe, though he had not done so before, and indeed had announced that he could not bear the very idea of doing so, or whether he had set off for a walk and fallen from the stretch of cliff that bounded the southern side of the small island would never be known. All his companions could tell was that he had vanished.

They all agreed that it had been an accident, just as Vanessa's death had been an accident; and if anyone other than Tamara realised how easy it would have been to cause it, nobody said so.

The shared longing to get away from what now seemed like dreadful imprisonment was left unvoiced except by Timothy Knipe. He was now speaking of dark forces ranged against the intruders to ancient Egypt's secrets. 'We have brought this upon ourselves. We should not be here. We are being punished. Too late now to remember the Pharaoh's curse.'

Ann Benson had been persuaded to swallow a few of the tranquillisers with which Max Solomon had been provided by the prudent Mr Osmond. The neatly packed medicine case, stamped on its blue leather with Camisis's pharaoh crest, was equipped with treatments for most physical emergencies short of death, and a typed sheet attached to the inside of the lid explained how to use them.

Max Solomon was willing but inept. Giles prescribed and Janet administered the medicine before helping the ravaged figure down the stairs and onto her bed. After a while the sound of gasps and sobs faded into silence.

'Thank God for that at least,' Timothy Knipe said. Ann Benson had been weeping continuously ever since first realising that her brother was missing. 'You wouldn't think she'd have tears or a voice left. I could do with one of those nice downers myself.' He stretched out his hand to the bottle. Nobody tried to keep it from him, and with a defiant laugh he swallowed two of the little capsules.

'They have really made sure you have everything,' Tamara said. She poked her finger inquisitively into the medicine chest. 'Lomotil, athlete's foot ointment, antihistamines, streptomycin.'

'You will find nothing here that could harm anyone,' Max said. He was unexpectedly back in control, and insisted on finding out when John Benson had last been seen. Had he left the barge before even going to bed last night? Were the clothes he had worn the previous day gone from his cabin? Had anybody heard anything?

Giles summoned Abdullah and Hassan. John Benson's bed had been slept in. Hassan had laundered a dirty shirt, as he did every day. The room had been used after the bed was turned down while everyone was at dinner.

Nobody had seen John Benson after bedtime the previous night. At least, nobody admitted to having done so.

The watchman had not noticed him going on shore; or said he had not.

'I suppose we all look as alike to them as they do to us,' Timothy Knipe said.

'If you are talking about our staff here, I must tell youu that none of them looks in the least bit like any other except for Yasser and Mohammet who are identical twins,' Giles told him.

'I can tell them apart,' Polly said. Tamara glanced around to see who noticed that give-away of the identity of a girl whose whole upbringing had been directed towards ensuring that she always remembered and could tell apart all the numerous people it would be her job to meet. Hugo was watching her, one eyebrow quizzically raised, but all the others were as indifferent to Polly's boast as unrelated adults usually are to the young.

That figured. All but Hugo were preoccupied, either by their own thoughts, like Max Solomon, or by their own selves, like Tim Knipe. None would have paid any real attention to Polly or to anyone else, except in the mirror of their self-absorption. Any apparent interest that Polly herself showed in the others was a practised performance too, not a genuine emotion. It was perhaps the strongest aspect of her conditioning, that she should always seem to care. That newly intransitive verb was probably dinned into her since the days when it would have been followed by a grammatical object: care about the people you meet, care about their reaction to you, above all care that you please them. But the veneer was cracking.

Probably, Tamara thought, all of us will show true selves through our disguises, unmistakably enough for them to be recognised even by people less perceptive than Vanessa had been. Soon everyone present would be able to write a candid exposure of the party at Qasr Samaan. Who first, she wondered, excluding herself?

Hugo Bloom had already recognised Polly. But now he was giving away a little of himself.

'I left the barge before breakfast,' he said.

'What did you . . .?'

'I've done it every morning. Get some exercise before the day hots up.'

'So did I,' Janet said. It was the first time she had spoken since breakfast. She was a silent, abstracted presence, going through the motions of being a member of a party. A pang of guilt stabbed Tamara's conscience. What should it matter to her if John Benson had disappeared? Her job was to keep a check on Janet. What was wrong with the woman?

'Well, did either of you see Benson?' Giles Needham said impatiently.

'Or each other?' Tim Knipe said, his voice slightly slurred, but still malicious.

'We went together.'

'An assignation, eh Janet?'

Hugo said, 'I have been jogging round the island every morning. As far as I know it was your first time, isn't that right, Janet? But it is why I am mystified about John. That first morning I said he ought to come too, but he was quite disgusted at the idea of being energetic so early in the day. Or later, actually.'

Tamara heard as clearly as if the words had been spoken aloud, John Benson's querulous voice announcing that he could not bear the idea of doing anything so uncivilised.

'And you saw no sign of him?' Max Solomon said.

'No. None. Did we, Janet?'

Janet flushed, an uncontrollable surge of colour staining her cheeks and watering her eye. Hugo put his arm around her shoulder, pulling her towards him with his hard, strongly tanned arm. He said, 'We might not have noticed anyway.'

'What a time to choose,' Timothy said. He pushed himself up from the canvas chair. 'I am going to lie down for a while. I find all this very distressing.' It was not clear whether he meant Vanessa's death, John's disappearance or Janet's defection. 'Perhaps I shouldn't have taken your tranquillisers.' Unsteadily he went below.

'Perhaps we should all take some,' Tamara said. 'Until rescue comes we could sleep the time away.'

15

Janet Macmillan was the first to break.

Tamara found her sitting on the peak of the island and said, 'Sister Ann, sister Ann, is there anybody coming?' But she needed no answer to know that there were no boats, there was no sign of other life on the wide water. The day was hot, hotter than ever in fact, and the wind was increasingly an irritant. It felt as though there was a fine grit on one's lips and teeth, tongue and eyes. The wind was bearing sand from the arid south where a yellowish haze like distant hills lay across the horizon. 'Day three . . . I wonder how many more.'

Janet was chewing at the skin around her fingernails. 'I can't take much more of this,' she muttered.

'If one looks on it as a chance to sunbathe . . .'

'I can't think what to do.'

Tamara knew a good deal about Janet. Janet knew little about Tamara. There could hardly be understanding between them. But Janet was unaware of any reserve between watcher and watched. She said, 'Your sister Alexandra. You are very like her.'

'So they say.'

'We have been friends for a long time. Since we were students together. Bristol. It seems like so long ago.'

'She still lives there.'

'I know,' Janet said. 'I went to stay with her once. Husband, children, dog, cat . . .'

'She gets a bit bored,' Tamara said.

'Yes, but it's so settled. Secure. She isn't going to have unexpected moral quandaries bounced at her.'

'Do you?' Tamara asked.

'I shouldn't be talking about it, least of all to you.' Janet looked over her shoulder. The two women were alone on their rocky prominence. Great birds wheeled overhead. 'They are wondering if we are carrion,' Janet said with a shudder.

'Oh, are they vultures? I should have known. They look as big as an albatross.'

'I follow your train of thought. You are afraid I'm going to fix you with my glittering eye?'

'Not afraid,' Tamara said.

'I ought to be afraid of you. I am in so much trouble with officialdom already,' Janet said.

'What do you mean?'

'Alex told me about you. I know what you are. I can almost guess why you are here.'

'All the same, I shan't do you any harm. Why don't you tell me if it would help to talk about it?'

There was silence for a few moments and when Tamara glanced at Janet again tears were washing down her face, a gush of water unaccompanied by sobs. She sniffed and wiped the back of her hand against her nose. She said, 'I have been such a bloody fool.'

Tamara waited. She had learnt from her lawyer father that people can't bear silence. He once told her they will fill it if you don't utter, and then they end up by telling you that you are a good listener, when what you have really been good at is getting them to talk.

'I shouldn't ever have come to Egypt,' Janet said.

Tamara said, 'You couldn't have known that Qasr Samaan would be such a disaster.'

'Oh, not that. In other circumstances I'd have loved it. No, because of Tim. Don't pretend you hadn't noticed about him and me. I came on this trip just because he was going to. Tim and that woman.'

'You wanted to spoil it for them?'

'Something like that. It was because of that book by Agatha Christie. It seemed fitting somehow, to dog their footsteps the way her character did. I think I even hoped that Tim would turn into the man in the book, plot with me to get rid of her – I don't know. I was crazy. I can't remember what I was thinking. I just got this idea, when I heard that Tim was coming here with Vanessa, I was determined to be here at the same time. I suppose I just wanted to make him sorry. Sorry for what he'd done to me.'

'Oh dear,' Tamara said.

'We lived together, you see. Nearly three years. I thought we were . . . you know.'

'I know.'

'And then he met that bitch. Vanessa. Funny, I always used to think that "never speak ill of the dead" was a description more than an injunction. I have never wanted to before, even about people I hadn't thought much of when they were alive. But Vanessa Papillon. Vera Pritchard. No wonder she changed her name. I feel very unforgiving about her. And it's so silly. He was a free agent. We always said so.'

'It's easy enough to say.'

'When I had friends with unhappy love affairs their problems were so predictable. And then it happens to you, and it's unique. I just didn't feel that he was free, not while I was still bound to him. I knew people weren't property, I didn't own him, but that was just all words. I wanted him. Funny, really, because now I wouldn't have him back gift-wrapped and repentant. But at the time I was damned if I would let her enchant him away so easily. Do you know, I really could have murdered her.'

'And did you?'

'I thought about it. Honestly. I went down to the cabins when everyone was having dinner that night and I thought, I could strangle her with a pair of nylon tights. Or bash her over the head with one of the digging tools. Even poison her. What with poor old Max's medicine chest and the unguarded photography store, it would be easy enough to find a lethal substance to force down someone's throat. But then Polly came down to fetch something and she looked so – so bloody silly. Young and ignorant and vain and frivolous, and I just thought, It's not such a long time since I was light-hearted like her, taking things as they came and leaving men instead of having them leave me. I looked at myself, and I just didn't know this hag-ridden female I'd turned into, seriously, or almost seriously considering committing a crime. Losing control. Forgetting about what really matters.' Janet giggled. She went on, 'And of course by then I was nursing my grievance. I was beginning to see through Tim too. You probably wonder what I ever saw in him.'

'He is very handsome.'

'You know the old saying.'

'You mean he doesn't do handsomely.'

'Right. But it took me some time to see it. When he first left, I was just obsessed with getting him back. Or getting my own back. I'm not sure which, now.'

'So you came on this holiday,' Tamara said.

'That was the main reason.'

'What were the others?'

'Work trouble.'

Tamara did not answer, until Janet went on, 'I shouldn't talk about it.' She pulled off her cotton hat, and wiped her hand over her forehead. 'It's so hot.'

'It's a bit much today. Do you want to go down?'

'No, I can't face them all. It's like some ghastly play, with one character being written out after another, it makes you wonder who is next. And that idiotic juvenile mooning around after Giles. She reminds me painfully of myself with Tim.'

'Or Hugo with you.'

'What on earth do you mean?'

'He is making it pretty obvious.'

'Yes, isn't he just! When he said about going for a jog this morning . . .' Janet wiped her face again. 'It isn't real though. Anywhere else . . . This place changes one. One needs something – someone.'

'I should say he'd fancy you anywhere,' Tamara said.

'Not me. My work.'

'I am afraid,' Tamara said, 'I don't exactly know what your work is.'

'You aren't supposed to. Nor is he. But it is all perfectly ridiculous.' With sudden energy Janet stood up, shook her skirts out and refolded them around her legs, and sat down again in a severe, upright position. 'I won't be gagged. Anyway, you're Alexandra's sister.'

'You are a biologist, aren't you?' Tamara prompted her.

'Not exactly. Physiologist. I work with the human brain. I have been studying the causes of epilepsy.'

'Electrical impulses of some kind?'

'That's right. But the trouble is that I have come across something that my bosses won't let me publish. Do you think there can be any justification for suppressing scientific discoveries, Tamara? After all, you are a sort of scientist yourself. You must have thought about it.'

Tamara temporised. 'It depends on the circumstances.'

'For instance, if you came across archaeological proof of something that was unacceptable and even dangerous. What if you could prove that black and white races descended from different species of primates and there really are inherent, ineradicable differences between them?'

'It would be political dynamite.'

'So would you suppress it?' Janet demanded. 'You must have been educated like me to believe that the free exchange of scientific results is a right. An axiom. A given, as an American friend of mine would call it. If he says this is one I'm going to take his word for it.'

'What about the pragmatic arguments? Perhaps one should suppress information about weapons, for instance. Or . . .' Tamara made a gesture as of one plucking a random notion from the air. 'What if one found a way of disseminating germs, so as to make it possible to wage germ warfare?'

'That is all very well, but the same information would probably tell you how to cure or prevent that very illness in its spontaneous form. It isn't for the scientist to judge the use of objective information. It never has been. All her duty is to publish it.'

'If she's allowed to.'

'That's the trouble. I had better not say what I've been working on, but Hugo knows about it and— '

'Did you tell him?'

'There didn't seem any point in not. I'm telling my American friend Cal. Anyway Hugo already had some idea of the line I was taking. I didn't remember him, but we had met a few months ago at a dinner party. Anyway, he says he'll take the risk of publishing it. The thing is, what my boss doesn't seem to understand, the good this can do would by far outweigh the harm it conceivably might, just possibly, most unlikely that it ever would, do. And while they dither about that, people are suffering who could be helped. Even cured.'

'I didn't know that Hugo could publish things. I thought he was a businessman.'

'He seems to have a finger in a good many pies. But for some reason he's very keen on this one. Of course he says that he's keen on me too.'

'Do you reciprocate?'

'Up to a point. To tell you the truth I am a bit frightened of him. He's very single-minded and – Good Lord. Do you hear what I hear?'

Tamara had noticed the noise several moments before, but hoped to hear more of Janet's confidences before mentioning it. She said, 'I can see something else in the water too. Rather closer by.'

16

The sound was that of a diesel engine distinguishable from that of the electricity generator by its deeper, less even firing.

The floating object was bobbing on the disturbed water not far from the south side of the island. It was a piece of twentieth-century flotsam, white expanded polystyrene that must once have served a useful purpose of its own; and now had become a raft to which what evidence remained of John Benson had become attached. It was not much more than half his pink shirt, an unmistakable garment whose breast-pocket trademark, a small green alligator, had become a disgusting parody. When Tamara and Janet pulled the trophy in, they found that the symbol was still there. The creatures, alligators, or crocodiles, perhaps even piranha fish, Janet suggested in a tone of hysteria, had left nothing else of its wearer, except a red bloodstain on a remaining fragment of collar.

The material evidence of John Benson's fate was only of equal interest to most of the party as the fact that Hugo Bloom had started the barge's engine. When Tamara and Janet came up with their morbid trophy Hugo was saying, evidently not for the first time, that he had not done anything, or, alternatively, that he did not know what he had done. 'I just pushed things in and out a bit,' he said with uncharacteristic imprecision. 'Pure fluke.' He broke off, as though with relief, at the sight of the two girls. Then he said, 'Oh my God.'

'It is a piece of John Benson's shirt,' Max Solomon pronounced, his voice and his sombre face like a Talmudic judge. 'He is really dead, then. There is no hope.'

But everyone had abandoned hope for John's survival before now. In this, as in Vanessa's case, death brought out the worst in the survivors, none of whom was really interested in anything except escaping from Qasr Samaan. Even Ann Benson, shaken awake from her drugged silence, accepted the proof of her brother's fate with a kind of apathy. Tamara, having rapidly packed her own few possessions, went to help Ann. She was sitting vacantly on the edge of her brother's bed, holding a pair of his socks as though she had started to roll them together and become distracted in the middle of the small task. Tamara took them from her and put them into the open grip. The dead man's clothes were heaped on the floor, the chest and the ends of the bed. He had brought far more than seemed necessary. Tamara began to fold trousers and underwear, and Ann watched her with dozy eyes.

'There is a shirt missing,' she said.

'Still in the laundry perhaps?'

'But the man brought the washing back.'

'Anyway, how can you be sure?'

'He had three of those Lacoste shirts. They were very expensive. He said he couldn't bear cheap imitations. I had to go to Harrods for them. A red one and a blue one and a pink one.'

'The pink one— '

'I know.'

'The blue one is here,' Tamara said and folded it into the suitcase, averting her eyes from the carnivore that was its trademark.

'I expect the servants have pinched the red one,' Ann said calmly. 'I told John he should have tipped them more.

But he always said he couldn't bear the kind of person who got good service by bribery.'

'I rather doubt . . .' Tamara began.

'But I know why he wouldn't. It was because Hugo could always outdo him. Do you know what I mean?'

'Did Hugo tip the staff here?' Tamara asked. It had not occurred to her to do so on arrival or since, though some notes were ready in her pocket, now that it seemed that moment had at last come.

'Lots. In fact lots and lots. Showing off, John called it. Throwing his money around. Even to the captain of the barge. It was like tipping a taxi driver. Hugo should have asked for his money back when the man was so inefficient. If he had made his beastly boat start we could have been away from here days ago and then John would never have died. Still,' she said with sudden, unexpected briskness, 'no use crying over spilled milk. I can say that now. John couldn't bear people who used clichés.'

'Can I help you with your own packing?' Tamara said.

'No need. There is hardly any to do. I never had as many things as John. He said I didn't need them, because he was the one who saw clients and buyers and had to convince them that he was a real authority. I wonder whether they will buy the things from me.'

'Do you think you will carry on your brother's business then?'

'Not likely. But I shall have to get rid of the stock if I'm to sell the house.'

'You have already decided to move?'

'Oh yes, for years and years, if John should die before me. I don't want to carry on looking after other people and being polite to them and sorting out their problems and pretending to care if they aren't feeling well or don't like the other guests or don't have enough time to practise their silly musical instruments or can't eat the food I cook.

Do you know what I mean? I want a flat with two bedrooms in a nice quiet part of London. All electric, no animals, no garden, just something cosy and snug that's easy to keep clean and warm. I've always wanted that, but I never had any money and I wasn't trained as a girl, not like you are nowadays. My parents wanted us to be creative, but I could never have played well enough for a professional career. I'd really like to have had a little shop, but John would never hear of it, not even when he started dealing in pictures and antiques. He always said that the atmosphere of Fernley provided them with authenticity.'

John Benson had brought a sizeable overnight bag as well as his suitcase. 'I'll put the washing things in here, shall I?' Tamara said; not that there seemed much point in packing a damp toothbrush and razor that nobody could, surely, ever wish to use again.

'If you want,' Ann said, getting into practice for not being polite to people.

Tamara unfastened the leather catches, and lifted out the waterproof pouch. Under it John Benson had stored his purchases – as, presumably, these apparently ancient objects were. Tamara could not tell whether the scarab had been through the digestive system of a turkey or whether the faience beads came from a pharaonic tomb or a workshop in downtown Cairo. John had acquired several miscellaneous objects, some of them, whatever their period, of great charm. Tamara would have liked to own the little alabaster dish with two girls' profiles carved on it in relief, or to have worn the lapis lazuli earrings and the cornelian intaglio ring.

Tamara upturned the bag onto the bed.

The hoard looked incongruous on the brown blanket, as though a robber had flung out his swag. In among the objects was a little wodge of folded paper which proved to be a copy of a page from Dengue's textbook on fakes. Tamara read it with interest. There was no way to recognise whether ancient Egyptian antiquities were genuine except by scientific processes in which they would be destroyed, and by 'feel'. Tamara understood about that at least, knowing the years of handling, feeling, examining, admiring, that were needed to enable a scholar to make judgements that were based on his or her own experience and that looked as though they were based on intuition.

No doubt the same applied to art and objets d'art. There would not be many people competent to doubt John Benson's assertions about the pictures he sold, or sufficiently suspicious to suspect the authentications he provided with them. It would be interesting to see whether his death confirmed his authority, or freed critics to query them. Vanessa would not even have waited for his death; she had shown that the libel laws existed for her to circumvent.

'John was going to get Giles to authenticate all those things,' Ann said.

'Really? I wasn't sure whether they were copies. I can't tell.'

'Nor could John, I shouldn't think. But Giles was to say they were real and write out certificates. John was going to ask him today.'

Tamara shovelled everything into the bag, telling herself that if buyers were fools enough to be taken in by John Benson, or now by his sister, they deserved to lose their investments.

A knock on the half-open door: Hugo Bloom. 'My poor girl, I am so sorry.' His Irish voice; by this time Tamara knew that his accent broadened in emotional moments. He put his arm around Ann, and wiped his own eyes. 'What can I say?' he said. 'How can I help you?'

'You have cut yourself,' Ann said.

'It's just an insect bite. But it's better to cover them in this country.'

'You know I have my first-aid certificate. Let me do it for you.'

'It really isn't worth it. At home you wouldn't even think of it. I'm just careful in the tropics. Listen, there is the siren.'

The harsh note blared across the water, and the passengers it summoned were as relieved to obey as the captain of the barge was to make it.

17

The Hotel Nefertiti in Abu Simbel was not patronised by package tours. It was able to accommodate the party from Qasr Samaan when Egyptair could not, and there they waited while Giles arranged for a bus or truck to carry them by road to Aswan. Max Solomon tried to book transport onwards to Cairo and London, frustrated by the caprices of the local telephones.

The system was not geared to independent travellers. At this, the height of the tourist season, no vacancies seemed to be available on any airlines or, as the travellers then discovered, in any hotels. An oriental king was paying a state visit to Egypt, and the Oberoi Hotel at Aswan and the Winter Palace at Luxor had been commandeered for him and his suite, decanting visitors with reservations into other hotels that were already fully booked.

Abu Simbel, known to nearly everyone as the site of a reconstruction, was revealed to be, behind the glories of the temple, an unconstructed yet already derelict town.

Egypt had been, if not European, then *sui generis*. So was Qasr Samaan, so utterly out of the world. Here, in the southernmost settlement of Upper Egypt, Tamara realised that she really was in Africa. Large women, their skins the glossy black of Nubia, their profiles fine and delicate, trod a stately way through filth and dust, carrying baskets of fruit or amphorae of water balanced at disconcerting angles on their heads. The houses needed no roofs here where rain was unknown, but rush matting was laid across the crumbling walls against the sun, and skinny goats stretched their necks to chew at its corners. Donkeys and camels jostled against battered cars and vans in the crowded streets. The reek of decayed food, and of animal and probably human excreta, was very powerful. Tamara wondered whether the whole world had once smelt equally disgusting, before the advent of drains, piped water and the internal combustion engine.

She waited by the door of the hotel to hear whether they must stay the night there, or could set off northwards. She watched a string of camels sway past on their way to market, pale, dusty creatures with petulant faces. The 'grown-ups' were slumped pessimistically on plastic chairs in the lobby. Polly was out on the step, and snatched back her offered hand as a camel's lip bared yellow teeth at it. Around her jostled a crowd of children holding out their hands, not to pat but to beg baksheesh. Behind them were their mothers, eyes peering above their veils, soon joined by a few men, who laughed as they spoke, obviously listing the charms (or otherwise) of the immodest woman. Their own wives or daughters would be shamed by the staring attention that Polly had been educated to attract. Her smile at the crowd was automatic and her hand began to make the familiar wave.

Giles stepped past Tamara to stand by the younger girl. 'Come inside,' he said. 'Suppose someone recognises you.'

She pushed past him and ran towards the only lavatory. Nobody would really have recognised her much photographed face in its present state. Giles looked at Tamara. His eagerness to be rid of the incubus the girl and his lack of interest in her as a troubled child were chilling. There came a point where single-minded pursuit of scholarship ceased to be commendable. Tamara said, 'All right. I'll cope.'

Polly was looking with dismay at the apology for a modern convenience. It had taken her mind off her own troubles if only for a moment. She said, 'I have never seen anything like it.'

'Or smelt,' Tamara said, holding her handkerchief in front of her nose.

Polly zipped up her trousers. 'Honestly, an earth closet would be better than this. You'd have thought . . .'

'If they had known you were coming they would have redecorated it,' Tamara said. Polly glanced at her with a practised, chilly stare.

She was young enough for her lack of make-up and generally scruffy appearance to be only a little disfiguring; but nature had not made her pretty. She was without the improvements she had been taught to assume and had applied throughout the stay at Qasr Samaan, until this last day. She had neglected a routine so necessary to her self-respect that she had observed it for every moment in Qasr Samaan, where, of all places, it might have seemed unnecessary.

Polly must have grown up believing that she mattered to the world. What else could have been the message of the pitiless attention, the continuous observation, that were inherent parts of Polly's life? Her unadorned face, marked by an infected insect bite on the forehead, was a symbol of the disintegration that was affecting the girl's own wilful personality.

Tamara, secure in the kind of complexion and features which others tried to mimic, saw with pity the other girl's low cheekbones, usually disguised with coloured powder; the mousy hair whose crafty auburn streaks were growing out; the ragged eyebrows and short-lashed, small eyes, that could be so convincingly improved with paintbrushes and pencils.

In the matter of her looks, if in nothing else, Polly was unlucky. She lived in an age which encouraged disguises;

but which provided the camera lenses to penetrate them. She would only look like a pretty princess in the pictures that had been adjusted to make her so. Still, changed or not, her face must still be a well-known one.

Tamara said, 'All the same, it might be more sensible if you kept your head down – literally. Don't you agree?'

It was automatic for Polly to crush impertinence, and her eyebrows began to rise before she suddenly crumpled into tears. 'I don't know what to do. What are they going to say when I get home? I'm going to be in dead trouble.'

'It could be a bit dicey.'

'And it wasn't even worth it in the end. If I'd come back engaged to Giles, they would have had to come round. Anyway, nobody was meant to know, except my family. Everything has gone wrong.' Polly knuckled her eyes and sniffed like a child. 'Whatever am I going to do?'

'You're safe enough here, anyway. Come on, we'll get something to drink and make a plan.'

For want of anywhere better, Tamara and Polly sat on the stairs leading up to the bedrooms already allotted to other travellers. Hugo and Janet had gone out to see what there was to be seen in Abu Simbel. Ann Benson was sitting on a mock leather bench in the bar, her head back against the wall and her eyes closed.

Tamara opened her capacious bag to find the aspirin.

'What's that?' Polly asked, pointing to a plastic bag.

'Sand. Soil.'

'Whatever for?'

'My father's garden. He sprinkles pieces of the world on the rockery. He's got some of the Holy Land, and the Grand Canyon, and even the Great Wall of China. He'll like this.'

'How interesting,' Polly said, with automatic warmth.

'So tell me. Did you think nobody would notice you'd gone?' Tamara prompted.

'I never thought it would get out. I left a note for my family explaining where I was. I was perfectly safe. Paula's family would never have let her go to Egypt if it hadn't been. I thought they'd say I had some mild illness, glandular fever or something, until I got back. I can't think what went wrong.'

'Obviously, your friend Paula never delivered the note; or somebody intercepted it. Somebody who took advantage of your being safely out of the way to do a bit of Robin Hoodery.'

'It must have been Paula. We were talking about it last term, what we could do to force the government to send some food. Someone had the idea of kidnapping me then. We all thought it was awfully funny.'

'It may have had the desired effect, of course. Would that help?'

'Nothing could help me now. But it is monstrous, you know; there are all those mountains of food that nobody wants being burnt or just thrown away while other people are starving. I spoke to the Prime Minister about it, actually.'

'Really? What did she say?'

'Just some waffle about it all being very dreadful. And then I got into trouble for talking about politics. But I don't think it's politics. It is simple humanity.'

'Perhaps Paula was justified then,' Tamara said.

'That's all very well.' Saving herself had become more important to Polly than saving the starving.

Tamara said cautiously, 'It might have come out even if Paula had delivered your letter as you arranged. Vanessa Papillon knew who you were.'

'Oh, I know. I was simply desperate. I simply did not know what to do.'

'What did you do?'

Polly looked at Tamara sideways, wondering whether to admit it. 'I thought of killing myself.'

'Not her?'

'No. I'm afraid that never occurred to me.' She sounded genuinely sorry. 'I sort of thought, if I just went to sleep and never woke up . . . There are several things that would have done it in the photography store. I even thought of putting selenium into my mineral water. Everyone would have been so sorry. The last time one of my family died young was before the first world war, and he was mental.'

'You changed your mind, did you?' Tamara enquired delicately.

'I wasn't too sure about the selenium. I knew it was poisonous, but it might have hurt. Anyway, Giles was up there, he wanted to know what I was up to. So then I thought I'd use pills. I knew Vanessa had lots, and I heard her borrowing more from Mr Solomon, so I nipped down after dinner to find them. And then of course it turned out to be unnecessary.'

Tamara recalled the flash of green fabric she had seen when she came out into the corridor the night Vanessa died. 'Do you mean you found her body before Timothy did?'

'I just thought she was ill. Honestly, I didn't know she was dying. I couldn't have known.' More sobs, more tears; Polly's heaves and gulps verged on the hysterical. She had let go of the rigid control suitable to her calling, which she had quite creditably maintained throughout the last few days. Polly had never been one to do things by half. Tamara shook her quite hard; and then, wondering whether it counted as *lèse majesté*, slapped her as she had slapped Tim Knipe on the night they were talking about. She said sharply:

'What do you mean? You had better tell me properly. I can't help you otherwise.'

The girl sobbed on, more quietly, beginning to control herself. Tamara hoped nobody would interrupt them. She waited, wishing that she were old enough to feel motherly or young enough to have fellow feeling for the girl's mixture of arrogance and immaturity. Eventually Polly gulped, 'I looked into her cabin, just to see if she was there, that was all, and she was being sick, and clutching her tummy, and I just thought it served her right. I was quite pleased. I thought she had Tutankhamun's revenge, you know? Honestly, if I had known she was seriously ill I would have . . .'

'I'm sure you would,' Tamara lied.

'Tamara, you won't tell anyone, will you? Can I count on you?'

'What did you do then?'

'The bell rang and I went up because it always seemed rude to be late when Giles and I were kind of host and hostess.' Having been foiled in her plan to poison herself, Polly went to preside at and eat a large dinner.

Tamara said, 'Was Giles the only one who saw you fiddling with the poisons and the mineral water bottle?'

'You know how everyone came up and down all the time.'

'Did anyone say anything? I don't remember because I wasn't there myself that night.'

'Of course, you were laid low, I was so sorry,' Polly said with the practised graciousness that she would never be able to disguise. But it was skin deep. It was impossible to believe that Polly could have seen Vanessa in her last agonies and really supposed her to be simply having an attack of gyppy tummy.

Was it possible to believe that she had caused it? Had she actually mixed her suicidal potion? Was she telling this story because Giles had told her that Tamara had the bottle that had been in Vanessa's room? Mercifully, Tamara thought, it is not my job to find out. But someone, somewhere, had better do so, before this mini-juggernaut is released into the world to enforce her will on other people and things.

Max Solomon was standing in the lobby, clapping his hands to awaken Ann and to attract the others. He looked pleased with himself. He had managed to lay on a bus. 'Well, I call it a bus. It won't be air-conditioned, and I have grave doubts of its springs. But it should get us to Aswan by morning. The first stage of our journey home.'

18

The full horror of their last few days hit the survivors of Qasr Samaan when they told someone else about them.

Sayeed had realised that the members of the Camisis party who had stayed in Aswan should not wait for their mysteriously delayed companions but catch their intended flight back to Cairo and from there home to London. He had escorted them to the International Airport, and seen them safely out of his country. He had then flown back to Aswan to await, with increasing mystification, the others' return.

'Miss Papillon? And Mr Benson too? Both? But this is dreadful news. More dreadful than I could have imagined. Naturally I was most anxious. I guessed, a strike perhaps; alas we have many strikes in my country. Also mechanical failures, though this, of course, you indeed experienced. But such tragedy, such disaster, that I did not picture. What grief!' He seemed genuinely sad; more so than those who had better reason to be. His elegant profile, the exact modern parallel of those so often depicted on tomb walls, his moist, large eyes, expressed emotions that in the others had been swallowed by impatience. 'I take it personally,' he said. 'that these accidents should have happened in my country!'

Tamara looked at the laden feluccas, tipped almost into the water by the fierce wind, and at the crowded terraces of the Old Cataract Hotel where she, along with far too many other foreigners, was waiting for news of reservations, flights and escape routes from the resort, and was only surprised that so few accidents happened in Sayeed's country.

Here, where Roman ladies once dreamed of recall to the hub of the fashionable empire, where nineteenth-century consumptives had breathed the dry and curative air, where diarists had rhapsodised over peace and beauty, an ill-assorted variety of world citizens elbowed through self-centred crowds. The wind that aggravated their irritability, swirled dust into their eyes and sun-hats from their heads. It dulled and darkened the fast-flowing Nile.

Giles had gone off on his own, saying that he would find the members of his team who must be waiting somewhere in Aswan for their return to Qasr Samaan.

Hugo, still indefatigable, said he was going to buy an early print of Philae that he had seen in an antique shop when they were in Aswan before. In the hotel lounge Polly, Timothy, Janet and Ann settled down in a corner and were soon asleep, their heads awkwardly propped against the wicker chair-backs.

They were politely ignored by the servants, who were dressed and behaved as though this were the set for a film about the old empire. Above the plants in their copper and brass pots, fans slowly turned, shifting the dusty air but hardly cooling it.

The previous night had been, by any standards, gruesome. The journey from Abu Simbel to Aswan had reduced the European passengers to fury, self-pity or dumb resignation in the mêlée of goats, chickens in coops, babies, cheerful but veiled women, disdainful and observant men, all clouded in a miasma of dust, diesel fumes and pungent snacks.

It had been left to Ann Benson to say, 'John wouldn't have been able to bear this.'

'If we know what you mean,' prompted Timothy Knipe. His own developing mannerisms were also secondhand, those of the star Vanessa had been. In public now he was ostentatiously bereaved. He carried Vanessa's hand luggage, and wore one of her filmy scarves. Tamara was not quite sure that he had not sprayed himself with her scent.

'Do you want to put that up on the rack?' Giles had asked, putting out his hand for the snakeskin case.

'I shall hang onto it. Vanessa's things are mine now. I am her heir.'

Could that be true? Or could Tim believe it to be true? He had not mentioned it before. If Vanessa had made a will in his favour he would have had a powerful motive to . . . But it was not Tamara's business. She shook her head, and then smiled at the dejected Nubian who had thought her gesture was directed at him. His company on the long drive was less demanding than Tim's would have been, and she woke at dawn, near Aswan, to find her own head on his striped cotton shoulder.

Sayeed laid his comforting hand on hers. 'You are tired. You are all tired,' he said. 'I go now to arrange a coach to take you northwards and you shall all sleep.'

There was no hope of getting on any flight. Numerous tourists who had been decanted from their hotel rooms to make way for a king were now queueing furiously at the airport for any conveyance that would get them away from Aswan.

More crowds besieged the telephones and telex machines. Max Solomon was in the queue. It had been agreed that he would do his utmost to get his party safely out of the country before Giles told the authorities of the two deaths at Qasr Samaan.

'We all know that they were accidents and you would be free to go in the end. But the bureaucracy, the hold-ups . . . you make a clean get-away. I'll carry the can.' Even those who did not realise that Giles's priority was to get Polly safely and secretly home, were only too eager to encourage his self-sacrifice.

'Not a word from us,' Timothy said firmly. 'Buttoned mouths, chaps, agreed?'

Tamara doubted whether discretion would be maintained for very long. If Max could not manage to get flights from Cairo there might be trouble. Nor would it be fair to Giles. He might plausibly be able to say that he had tried and failed to keep his guests available for questioning but that they had left before the police could get to them. If he was shown to have delayed while material witnesses were still in Egypt, things would be very tough for him, though Tamara did not doubt that he would get away with it. Where his work was concerned, Giles had a tenacity that was probably invincible. There was only one thing in which he was interested and monomaniacs tended to get their way in the end.

But the immediate question was whether Max Solomon would be sufficiently single-minded. His plan had been to send messages to Camisis and leave Mr Osmond to pull what strings he could. He was going to try Egyptair and the British Embassy in Cairo too, but without optimism.

Tamara found that he was near the front of the telex queue. He was waiting between a robed Nigerian and a uniformed Japanese courier. She scribbled down some letters and numbers. 'It is a priority code. If you read it to the people at the Embassy it might help.'

'I see.' Max looked at he scrap of paper, and then up to meet Tamara's non-committal gaze. 'So my friend Professor Thomas is not in domestic trouble after all? That is good news.'

'I haven't said a word.'

'It is not necessary. But I will dictate your signal.'

'Let's just hope it works.'

Another busload of tourists was being unloaded at the front of the hotel. They pushed each other aside to get to their luggage. Some Italians were getting into a coach, chattering cheerfully. A miscellaneous group was standing around their courier; all carried bags that matched her identifying pennant. Between them cars backed and edged, their turning space obstructed.

The large, but not large enough, parking space of the hotel was edged by flowering bushes and trees, from which blossoms were being stripped by the relentless wind. By the jacaranda tree on the way through to the swimming pool, Janet was standing with Hugo Bloom. He put his arm round her and kissed her cheek. He pointed down towards the town. Then he turned to enter the hotel, and Janet began to walk down the sloping driveway.

I had better go with her, Tamara thought.

Two men were coming towards Janet. They parted to let her pass between them. She seemed to stumble, and one of them caught her by the shoulder. A taxi whose engine had been running, swooped beside them, and the two men dragged Janet Macmillan into the rear seat between them. By the time Tamara had dodged through the buses and the tourists, and run across the forecourt, the taxi, and its passengers, had disappeared from view.

19

There were no empty taxis. There were no cars to commandeer, only buses and ignorant visitors. No help was at hand. Nor could Tamara be certain that she needed it. She suddenly felt utterly weary, the sleepless night of travel catching up with her, and she wondered whether she was imagining or even dreaming what she had seen – or what she thought she saw. Had Janet really been bundled unwillingly, perhaps even unconsciously, into a car, here, of all places? It is idiotic, Tamara thought, my mind runs on melodrama. I see a peaceful event and introduce poisoned umbrella tips, or knock-out jabs. It is a professional deformity, and I only gave way to it because I didn't have enough sleep.

But then, where had Janet gone? Who had she gone with? Tamara played the scene through her memory again. Janet had been greeted by Hugo. He kissed her. Why had he done that? They had been together for days, would be for more days – what had that deliberate salute, not the kiss of a lover but a formal, quick cheek-to-cheek been for? It was as though he were marking her out, saying 'this is my woman'; or perhaps, 'this is the woman'. An identification, pre-arranged, for fellow conspirators who needed to be certain that they got the right person.

Janet had said that she was almost afraid of Hugo. What else, apart from the fact that he found her physically attractive, could interest him in her? Only her work. Only the work that she had discussed with Hugo; about which he had questioned her; which he had offered to publish for her.

Max Solomon was no longer in the telex room. Giles Needham had not come back to the hotel. Sayeed had disappeared. Ann Benson, Polly and Timothy Knipe were still dozing, lucky to be able to sleep their waiting time away among the pierced screens and old colonial furniture of the cool-tiled hotel.

Hugo Bloom was at a curlicued white table beside the swimming pool. A waiter, barefoot and wearing a red fez, had just brought him a tall glass, frosted with ice, and he took a long swig.

Tamara went to sit with him. He waved at the waiter. 'Fruit juice? No? One mineral water for the lady please. Look, Tamara, I have found this print of Philae. Charming, don't you think?' It was a mass-produced reproduction of one of David Roberts's watercolours. Except for being on thicker paper, it could have been torn from a Sunday newspaper's colour supplement. John Benson would not have approved. His own fake would have been more convincing.

'I was looking for Janet. Have you seen her?'

'Isn't she asleep up on the terrace?'

The moment of revelation was as exciting as stout Cortés's on that peak in Darien. It was for this heady surge of triumph that Tamara did her secret work. But her face was not the mirror of her mind.

'Is she? I didn't look. What a bad night they must all have had in that bus. I slept quite well myself.'

Not a conquistador; a bird catcher . . . a lion hunter . . . a big-game stalker? Softly softly catchee monkee, she thought, making a good mix of her metaphors.

'I wonder whether we shall manage to get away tonight,' Hugo said.

'Sayeed thought he would be able to organise at least a minibus; or a couple of taxis.'

'We'll be reduced to sleeping out on the corniche otherwise.'

Did Hugo suppose they could set off without Janet, in the same way that they were without Vanessa and John? Would he perhaps create evidence that she had left of her own free will; or that she, like Vanessa and John, was dead?

Tamara thought of John Benson, perhaps still with the tattered remnants of his red shirt clinging to what was left of his flesh. And she thought of the ingenuity that had enabled someone, his murderer, to take the paler shirt, and stain it with red, and arrange that it should be found in the water at Qasr Samaan. They might all be there still, if such proof of his death had not turned up. It was important to someone, to whomever had made those arrangements, that they should get away.

But here, and now, was Hugo sure that Janet would be safely – and uncomplainingly – returned? What was the connection between them? Was there a connection at all? Ten little Indians went out to play . . . at this rate, there would soon be none.

She kept the desultory conversation going. 'It seems hotter than ever.'

'Yes. The khamsin doesn't help.'

'It will be almost nice to get home to rain.'

But Tamara could not go home without Janet. This was a mystery that really was her business.

'Pity there is no chance to go and see the Aga Khan's tomb,' Hugo said. It was invisible through the cloud of dust that swirled over the desert and the water.

'It would have been nice to see the Tombs of the Nobles too,' she agreed.

Hugo Bloom. Tamara tried to remember what she had learnt about him in her quick pre-trip briefing, but nothing gave her a clue as to his behaviour and motives now.

'And the monastery of Saint Simeon,' Tamara added.

Hugo was Irish. Could that have anything to do with it? He didn't look it though. He looked remarkably like the Egyptians themselves.

'I'm quite happy to give Saint Simeon a miss. I've had enough of deserts for the time being,' he said.

If Hugo Bloom had set himself to get the details of her discovery from Janet, in bed or out of it, while they were out of the world at Qasr Samaan, and had not managed it . . .

'Can I order you another drink?' she said.

Had he made fail-safe arrangements for acquiring the information? But what did he want it for, so badly as to commit crimes for it?

'The wind makes one quite parched. I'd love one. What about you?' Hugo replied.

Was Hugo the perpetrator of those other crimes? He had the opportunity to poison Vanessa, and to push John Benson into the deep lake. Everyone had had the opportunity.

'I'll have some coffee, I think,' Tamara said.

That would anchor him a little longer, give Tamara more time to think. It was a pity that her brain felt so soggy. Sharpen your wits. Think.

Hugo was sitting by this pool in perfect idleness. He did not glance at his watch. His body language did not express any tension or impatience.

'May I join you? You both look so comfortable and relaxed.' Max Solomon, remarkably imperceptive for a man of his trade.

'Any luck on the transport front?' Hugo asked, waving for the waiter.

Hugo could have ensured that there was no transport away from Qasr Samaan. Ann Benson had mentioned his tipping the barge captain. Had he bribed him to keep the engine out of order while he worked on Janet?

'I am waiting to be called back. I will have mango juice, please.'

When the message was sent to Wadi Halfa Hugo must have realised that he could not keep them marooned any longer. He went over to the demobilised barge to do something mechanical – he said. He had probably done something financial instead.

'I have had a most interesting encounter,' Max said. 'One of the older members of the hotel staff, a local man. He was telling me that as a child his great friend was his neighbour, a Jewish boy. It seems that many Jewish families lived here, forty, fifty years ago, and emigrated for the usual reasons.'

'To Israel?' Tamara asked.

'Presumably. Certainly this man did, for he came back with an Israeli package tour as soon as it became possible after the Camp David accord and reforged his old friendships. Now his grand-daughter and my new friend's grandson have become close. After all that had happened.'

'That's a cheering tale,' Hugo said.

'I thought so.'

Bloom. It is not an Irish name. He must be Jewish; James Joyce's Irish Jew was called Bloom too.

'Didn't Anwar Sadat come from Aswan himself?' Tamara said.

'Perhaps he too had a Jewish friend when he grew up here. It may have made it easier for him to talk to Begin,' Hugo said.

'When I was here in nineteen eighty-one, with my dear wife, Sadat's photograph was all over the place. He had a villa here.'

What had Mr Black said when he explained about Janet's work? 'You could knock out every tenth man across disputed borders . . .' He had not been more specific, and Tamara's thoughts had jumped to the border between Northern Ireland and Eire. Hugo Bloom might have thought of that too; but perhaps he had visualised every tenth Israeli soldier on guard over the Golan Heights or the River Jordan, temporarily blinded or paralysed . . . chaos . . . invasion, destruction and – ever present in a Jew's fear – genocide. If Hugo knew what Janet had developed, he could well have decided that any risk was worth taking to get it.

'Excuse me, I must just . . .' Tamara went in as though towards the lavatory. Ann and Polly were even more deeply asleep. Ann's jaw was open and she was dribbling. Timothy was snoring. Polly's head was buried on her folded arms. Her hair straggled across the table. Tamara went outside again.

'I can't think what has happened to Janet,' she said.

'Isn't she with the others?' Max asked.

'I think we had better look for her.'

'No need, surely?' Hugo said. 'She's bound to be back here before we leave.'

Does that mean that he has managed to ensure our departure is delayed as he did before? Or does he know exactly how long his colleagues will take to get everything out of Janet? Either way, the implication was that Janet was either not going to remember what had happened to her, or that she would be persuaded not to complain of it, or that she would not live to tell her tale.

'Look at the storks,' Max Solomon said.

There must have been several thousand of them, great white creatures in an incredible flock, flapping northwards. Hugo looked at them through steady binoculars. With his arm raised a sticking plaster showed pink against the brown. Tamara thought again of the blood on John Benson's rags of sport-shirt.

'It was amazing to see the birds migrating out of Africa while we were at Qasr Samaan,' Hugo said.

Cool or genuinely not nervous. What could the man have arranged, on that quick so-called shopping trip into the town? His colleagues must have been all ready to do whatever they were doing. This was a very smooth operation. Hugo must have discussed it beforehand, when they were all in Aswan before going down to Qasr Samaan. His insurance.

'The birds were my wife's great pleasure when we were here before. Ornithology was her passion.'

Max could talk about her again. He's changed, Tamara thought. Earlier on he would only utter polite nothings, like when he discussed the weather or the tat the old ladies had amassed in the market. He had been so kind and so uninvolved, admiring Lady Gentle's appallingly crude replicas of Nubian ivories, and Ann Benson's necklace of fake turquoise, and even Hugo's brass tray that was probably imported from Taiwan.

'When we are back in England you must come and see my Audubon Birds of America,' Hugo said.

'You have the originals?'

'Yes, I bought them at Sotherans about ten years ago.'

A man who treated himself to the Audubon birds, neither wanted an obvious fake of a David Roberts temple, nor a brass tray from Taiwan. Tamara leant back and allowed her eyes to fall closed. She knew what she looked like to the two men – candid, unsuspicious and unworldly.

She worked backwards in her memory. They had been sitting in the garden of the Oberoi Hotel, shaded by lush acacia and eucalyptus trees. Hibiscus flowers floated in small vases on the tables. Hugo had walked up from the boat that ferried hotel guests over to the town. Lady Gentle was twitting him, in a kind of heavy-handed, elderly flirtation. She had seen him in the bazaar and accused him of having a lady friend there. That tinkling, memsahib's voice. 'In Sharia el Suq, just beside the shop where they sell ebony models of feluccas.'

Tamara opened her eyes. She put her straw hat on her head.

'I shall go for a stroll,' she said. 'No. Don't come. I just feel like looking around a bit.'

20

Tamara met Giles on the steps into the main hotel. He had moved on to the next stage, the real thing in his life, and looked surprised to be reminded of the previous one. He said, 'Still here?'

'You found your team?'

'They are raring to go. We managed to get onto this evening's flight back to Abu. Fletcher has had a new idea about section seven-B, he's been talking to a bloke from Qasr Ibrim where they had a similar problem. We think the thing is to extend the cutting to the east.'

'I'm looking for Janet,' Tamara said.

'Janet?' Giles's capacity for expelling unnecessary lumber from his mind demonstrated the reason for his success in his own subject. If Janet were the remains of a woman from an early dynasty, she would have a more secure place in his memory. 'Pity you can't come back with us and see. It should be interesting.'

Interesting, no doubt; but what had waited millennia for discovery could wait a little longer. Janet Macmillan could not.

Standing two steps above Giles, Tamara could look into, rather than up to his face. It all seemed rather a pity; the chunky brown skin, green eyes and delightfully zig-zag mouth were wasted on a man who was bored by the living and enthralled by the dead. He was quick-tempered and intelligent, at least about what obsessed him. As far as her present purpose was concerned, he was completely useless. She turned and went back into the building.

In the privacy of a lavatory cubicle, Tamara took her polythene bag of desert sand from her overnight case. To it she added a chunk of rock from the garden of the Cataract Hotel. She fed the full bag into the toe of a sock and hefted it experimentally. It would do – unless it broke the strap of her shoulder-bag first. She had brought some nylon stockings, but worn neither them nor her socks in the heat. They were an indispensable part of her equipment.

Tamara found Timothy Knipe awake and about to soothe his impatience with alcohol. It was not hard to induce him to come down towards the town with her. He began, as she had intended, by misinterpreting her motive but it was easy to brush off his roving hands while keeping his usually roving attention fixed on her. It was also easy, as she had not expected, to press him into her service.

'The thing about being a poet,' he explained, 'is that nothing is improbable.'

'You can believe six impossible things before breakfast?'

'No problem, especially when someone who looks like you asserts them.' The difficulty was not going to be persuading, but restraining him. He walked beside Tamara with a swashbuckling stride, like a man setting out to glorious battle, and the crowds parted to let him through. With a small part of her mind, Tamara thought about the unreliability of appearances. Giles and Tim both belied theirs; but then of course, so did she. Tim, who looked like a warrior, would do very well for watching and waiting. Tamara would cope with any necessary action herself.

The bazaar was very busy, and in its narrow streets the dusty wind was less uncomfortable.

'Look casual,' Tamara said, and she and Tim strolled between the shops and stalls, glancing from side to side at the heaps of powdered spices, the meat dripping its thin blood into the pavement runnels, the lengths of woven and cotton materials, the ivories and ebonies and other exotica from the dark continent. Arabs, Nubians, Africans, tourists from all over the world and of all colours jostled through the crowded alleys. Police in their sand-coloured uniforms walked in pairs, hands on revolver butts, their opaque dark glasses swinging from sight to sight.

Tim did not want to wait on his own by the window full of ebony models of feluccas.

Tamara said, 'You seem too formidable. Let me prowl a bit, I'm obviously harmless.'

A man in a business suit was leaning against the wall, just inside the door from which Lady Gentle had once seen Hugo emerge. He was certainly more highly trained than she, with combat experience she could hardly imagine, but her appearance gave Tamara that instant's advantage; and he was not expecting trouble. She entered looking at once tentative and curious. He turned and saw her, and she gasped prettily and clapped her open palm over her mouth. She went on walking forward. She said, 'Oh gosh! I didn't know – I say, do you understand English?'

It was a narrow corridor, once white-washed and now dingy. It was lit from above, through holes in the roof which had never been mended. At the far end was a closed modern door. It fitted far better between its jambs than it probably had two weeks earlier. Wood shavings lay on the floor near it.

The man stretched his arm to the other wall to bar her way. He smiled; a good-looking tough, with steady eyes and clean, short-nailed hands and white, even teeth. He was not labelled by anything except his self-confidence. Tamara was sure he was an Israeli. He spoke in almost unaccented American:

'Yes, I speak English.'

'Oh great. So many people here don't. Actually you've got a wonderful accent.' Tamara went on moving forward as she chattered. His outstretched arm was above her head and she hardly needed to duck to get under it. He grabbed at her shoulder.

'There's nothing here. This is private.'

Tamara turned round, facing him and the street. She smiled up at him. 'What a shame. It's such fun exploring. Everything is so quaint. Darling,' she called, 'do come and have a look in here.'

The man whirled round.

Standing on tiptoe, Tamara swung her cosh neatly behind his ear just as she had practised during training on a dummy with chalk marks that indicated the vulnerable points. The man punctually and almost silently collapsed to the floor. Tamara tied his hands and feet together and to each other behind his back with one nylon stocking and used the other to gag and blindfold him. She removed the small revolver from his shoulder holster and put it in her own pocket.

The new door was locked. Tamara tiptoed back to the outside entrance and called to Tim. He came towards her as willingly as a dog. Tamara put her hand over his pursed lips to stop him whistling at the sight of her victim. She whispered, 'It's just a knack. Honestly. I go to self-defence classes. That's why you might as well leave all this to me. I think Janet's in there.'

One could read in his changing expressions the rival emotions of cowardice and the desire to show off. Tamara did not give him time to decide between them. 'Give me a leg up, and then stay just outside again. Make sure the other man doesn't escape with her.'

He heaved her upwards, and she scrambled through a ragged hole onto the roof. It was piled with rubbish; an open-air lumber room. On neighbouring flat roofs goats, chickens and children seemed to lead their daily lives. All the same, she had better hurry in case somebody noticed how unlike the usual roof-dwellers she seemed.

There was new glass above the locked room, but it was propped a little way open with a long pole. It must be unendurably hot inside. The second man had taken off his jacket and his gun harness and left them on the back of the only chair. He was standing over Janet's recumbent form. She lay on a straw pallet, her hands by her side and her feet together. A syringe was on the floor beside her. Though her eyes were closed, her lips lazily moved. She was answering the questions the man put to her. He was crouched by her side. With one hand he held a recording machine close to her mouth, with the other he repeatedly wiped his dripping forehead. His back was to Tamara, and she was above him.

Tamara pointed the gun, first at the man's head and then at his chest. But she did not want to kill him.

If the gun did not shoot true she might regret her restraint. She took careful aim, and shot him through the right wrist. It was a sophisticated new weapon and made a noise no louder than the military aeroplanes in formation overhead. The man's scream sounded like a cock crowing. She shot again, as the man staggered backwards, through the shoulder blade. How I hate guns, she thought, as she lifted the skylight and dropped through the opening onto the floor, and how I hate blood.

The man was not unconscious, but immobilised and concentrating on his own agony. Knocking him out with her sandbag seemed almost like a kindness. Tamara wiped her own sweaty prints off the gun with her own shirt and dropped it on the floor. She took the cassette out of the recording machine and put it and the spare one in her pocket.

Tamara unlocked the door. The guard was conscious, but she had gagged and tied him well enough for it not to matter. She stepped past him and hissed to Timothy to come in. He would cringe and heave at the sight of the blood. He would be frightened by what he was involved in. But Janet was several inches taller and pounds heavier than Tamara. Alone she could not move her. Tim was strong enough to support an almost inert woman and it was for that function that Tamara had brought him along.

21

'Timothy Knipe kept well clear of me after that,' Tamara said.

Mr Black said, 'I expect you had frightened him off.'

Tamara had frightened herself off too. She realised it on the way home, during the flight from Aswan to Cairo.

She never did discover which luckless passengers lost their seats on the aeroplane when the magic code number did its trick, nor how some official at the British Embassy had arranged for the survivors to leave the country without further formalities.

Hugo Bloom was not with them.

He had been on the steps of the New Cataract Hotel when a garry pulled by a dejected horse delivered Tamara, Tim and a still hardly conscious Janet. He hurried into the town himself, presumably to find out what had happened, and was arrested, red-handed – as it must have seemed to the authorities – beside his putative victims. News was still awaited that (or whether) Giles Needham had also been arrested and put in beside him. Tamara was prepared to believe that Giles would ignore, and even forget, the fact of two dead English people at Qasr Samaan; and if the computers never turned up the fact that Vanessa Papillon and John Benson had entered but not departed from Egypt, he might never be reminded.

Nobody from the consulate had yet seen Hugo. Mr Black wondered whether he was waiting for rescue by the Israeli army. 'They ought to show him some gratitude, short of a commando raid. That information would have been quite some present.'

Would was the operative word. Mr Black and Tamara looked at the copy of the American *Journal of Mechanical Medicine* that lay on the desk in front of him. Janet's discovery was the subject of the leading article. Her friend Cal had done her proud.

'She dumped the problem on him so he decided what to do and did it,' Mr Black said.

'An inconvenient and uncharacteristic case of promptness in the Egyptian postal services.'

Janet had given her letter to an Arab to post at Dendera, realising that mail left on the ship to be posted was likely to be seen and wondered about by other passengers. 'She isn't as naïve as I thought,' Tamara said. 'She guessed from the very start that someone was there to keep an eye on her. It could have been anyone who booked the trip after she did, but I think she probably eliminated the Bensons straight away.'

'She assumed it was Hugo Bloom,' Mr Black said.

'In the role of agent provocateur? No, I rather think she guessed it was me. Don't forget my sister had been indiscreet about it in the past.'

'There are certain drawbacks to this small worldness of the life people like you lead.'

'People like me! What on earth do you mean? It was pure coincidence that Janet knew Sandra.'

'One of those coincidences that so regularly pops up in the life of you second-, third-, fourth-generation intellectuals.'

Tamara knew that he was teasing; in his own world of senior civil servants and ex-regular officers there was a far more powerful network than any that intellectual or social snobbery could provide.

'Anyway,' she said firmly, 'the upshot is that the whole excursion was a wasted effort.'

'On Hugo Bloom's part?'

'On mine.'

'Completely wasted? You have seen the Sphinx. You made some interesting friends. Attractive, too.'

'That, unfortunately, is quite misleading. The phrase "handsome is as handsome does" might have been coined about Giles Needham in the first place.'

'Your work was good,' Mr Black said. He sounded indulgent. 'You must be glad you rescued Janet. It was well done.'

But it was not well done. Tamara was ashamed to remember herself as a cold fighting machine. She had disabled two men. 'I could have saved her without the brutality,' she muttered.

'How? Without exposing the very secret you stopped her telling?'

'But the point is that she had already told it. And even if she hadn't, there must be something I could have done. I didn't stop to think.' It was the picture of herself as a rapid, decisive automaton from which her memory shied away.

In the jet that took them back to London Janet had been unwell, probably suffering the after-effects of whatever drug her captors used to loosen her tongue. Tamara had been sympathetic and helpful; and in a part of her mind felt that she had no right to minister to the sick. She was tainted by her own passionless expertise. 'It wouldn't be so bad if I'd even felt angry. If I had acted in hot blood. But I didn't. It was just the next thing to do.'

'You were calm and sensible.'

'That is a contradiction in terms, Mr Black. It is inherently *not* sensible to use force except in self-defence.'

'Or in defence of your protégée.'

'You may be able to justify what I have become in verbal logic. But I feel . . . corrupted. That's the only word for it.'

'That is the nature of involvement in affairs. The only true innocents are those who make sure they never know what other people are doing for them.'

'To them,' Tamara said.

'The victims?'

'I am not sure that anyone would ever have called Vanessa Papillon innocent. And as for John Benson . . .'

'A forger.'

'And a victim.'

'But not, it seems, Hugo Bloom's.'

Max Solomon had not resumed his diary writing at Qasr Samaan after emerging from his creative seclusion. But he had described his last days there to his son Jonty, for whom his father's words were among the few facts he could record in a mass of speculation.

Unlike Tamara herself, Max Solomon slept badly on that last night, and heard his neighbours' night noises through the cosmetic partitions that separated the cabins. John Benson had snored, Ann Benson ground her teeth. And Hugo Bloom had spent the whole of the night with Janet Macmillan. They had made and could have made little secret of it. In the morning they had parted for no more than ten minutes, met fully dressed in the passage and gone up to have a quick jog and then breakfast together.

Max had heard other footsteps on the stairs before that; but not Hugo's. He listened to the repeated scraping of Giles Needham's matches as he lit his morning pipe. He listened to John Benson snorting himself awake and performing uninhibited morning rituals. He heard him go up the stairs, muttering about what he could not bear; and Ann Benson say 'John?', unanswered, before she resumed her rhythmic grinding. He heard Giles, always first to resume the day's duties, go up; and the swish of a woman's skirt in the passage and her soft footsteps. He had not looked out of his door. Max thought it could have been Tamara he heard, or Polly. That was at least ten minutes before Janet and Hugo amorously separated to get dressed, and twenty before anyone else emerged.

'Polly,' Mr Black said.

'She was already in the saloon when I went up there with Janet and Hugo, but she was usually there before the rest of us. I didn't think anything of it,' Tamara said.

'You were so sure that Hugo was your man.'

'I am afraid I was.'

'Not entirely your fault,' Mr Black said kindly. 'You couldn't have known how useful to him the Bensons were. He would have wanted them alive. His Israeli masters—'

'I think friends would be a better word,' Tamara said.

'As you like. But I told you that our colleagues have worked out how he was spying on Fernley. Why it never occurred to anyone that the Bensons next door were providing the perfect base for checking on what goes on there, I really can't think. But heads are rolling like billiard balls.'

'And whose head will roll for Vanessa Papillon and John Benson?' Tamara asked. She faced the facts in her own mind. 'They are dead, almost certainly murdered. You can't get away from it. It happened. It's where fairy tales meet real life. Unless you see yourself, ourselves, as fairy godmothers.'

Mr Black got up from his chair and walked to the window. His office had recently been moved from Fortress House in Savile Row to another branch of the civil service maze; now he could look out on Whitehall.

'I prefer this,' he said.

'Soldiers to tailors?' Tamara said.

'I like processions. I like ceremonies. I like royal occasions.' The window was bullet-proof and mirrored reflections, rather than showing what was inside. There was modified triple glazing, to prevent vibrating words from being picked up by well-aimed microphones. The room (larger and more luxurious than the one he had had before) was checked three times a week for eavesdropping devices.

He said, 'I honestly don't know what's to be done.' It was unlike Tom Black to admit to anything but omniscience and even omnipotence.

Tamara said, 'About Janet?'

He looked surprised, as though he had forgotten the original purpose of Tamara's mission. 'That's over with, spilt milk. It will be up to the defence boffins to find an antidote. Win some lose some, as they say. No, not that.' He shuffled around in the papers on his desk. It was affectation. He had never been known to lose or even mislay anything. 'It's the analyst's report on the stuff you brought back in that mineral water bottle. And, incidentally, the Lacoste shirt. It was stained with ink.'

'I thought blood would have come off in the water. But Hugo had a cut on his hand.'

'A plaster to cover spilt red ink, I should think,' Mr Black said. 'But there was poison in the mineral water. You were right about that.'

'Selenium from the chemical store? Or Max Solomon's sleeping pills?'

'No, arsenic. It was in an extraordinary compound of ingredients. It wouldn't be permitted here or in the United States, even as a skin lotion. It is sold plastered with warnings. Not to be taken internally, use with care, keep away from children. Claims to remove wrinkles, very expensive, imported from the Far East. A magic potion.'

'Taken from Vanessa's own collection,' Tamara said, 'but surely not by her.'

It could have been any of those present on the dormitory barge at Qasr Samaan who put the poison into Vanessa Papillon's bottle of mineral water, as Tamara had realised at the time. Whether it was indeed a drink from that bottle that had poisoned her could not now be established, short of a post mortem to find traces of arsenic in the body. There was no need for one.

Tamara had followed this trail of conjecture before, several times, with the boring repetitiveness of any thoughts that are incapable of resolution.

Vanessa had died as a result of poison; she could have committed suicide. The other members of the party had accepted that her death had been accidental. One of them, however, had almost certainly caused it. Any of them could have done so. Tamara had veered between suspecting all, any and none of them. 'How could one prove it?' she muttered.

'Get hold of the body, have a post mortem. Take evidence from everyone who was at Qasr Samaan. Bounce a confession.'

'But who would? The British police? The Egyptian? It's unthinkable. I don't know what you are going to do about it,' Tamara said.

'I?' replied Tom Black. 'My dear Tamara – what are you?'

22

To a certain extent Tom Black was right. He usually was. Tamara did live in a small world – at least, as to the aspect of her that the larger world recognised. It was seldom very hard to arrange to meet people who were second-, third- or fourth-generation educated. Somewhere there would be a more or less elaborate maze of common acquaintances, through which she could find her way to the desired centre. It was simply the result of living on a small island with an archaic system of education.

The approach to Paula Crosse was simple. Professor Crosse was a colleague of Thea Crawford, who had been Tamara's tutor and was now her friend. His daughter was at home with them, near Buriton in Cornwall. She could not be locked away in the privacy of a Scottish castle.

Polly, on the other hand, had been sent north, away from reporters, photographers and curious eyes. It was either a punishment or a protection depending on which story one believed or on which of her parents was talking. They thought that Paula was more at fault than Polly. They would have liked to have their daughter's commoner friend clapped into the Tower of London for treason.

The Crosses were as much proud of their daughter as they were angry with her. They thought the cause for which she had cheated first her friend and then her government justified any minor misbehaviour. Polly's family should think itself lucky, Mrs Crosse said, that Paula was not interested in publicity.

As a matter of fact, Paula would have liked to get the credit for those plane-loads of supplies. She wanted to believe that she herself had been the saviour of the lives the food had, one presumed, saved.

By this time a good many of her friends knew what she had done. It would not be long until the story was public knowledge. Would Polly still be thought a heroine?

Tamara Hoyland, who suspected that Polly was a criminal, was taken to the Crosses' house by Professor Thea Crawford. Thea had listened to much of Tamara's story with commendable detachment; she was in the final stages of a long book about European connections with Britain in the Iron Age, and the doings of a Hanoverian princess were of far less interest to her than that Tamara had brought her an accurate drawing of a relevant sherd of pottery in the Aswan museum. She clearly felt that driving Tamara five miles out of town to the Crosses' place was payment for it. It was not ungenerous. Thea had to pretend that she was buying supplies from Mrs Crosse's trout farm for a dinner party as excuse for a call she could not otherwise plausibly make. Tamara, introduced not as Dr Hoyland but by her first name alone, put on her ingénue face, and said she had met Paula at a party in Oxford and would go out in the garden to hunt for her. She would not have been surprised to hear Mrs Crosse telling her to go outside and play.

Paula's penance was to gut and fillet fish.

'Mother's expanding into smoking and pickling,' she said gloomily, holding out her slimy hand as evidence that she could not shake Tamara's. 'I am getting used to the smell, but you'd probably rather go outside.' Outside was windy and damp.

'Typical Cornish weather,' Paula said.

'It's welcome after Qasr Samaan,' Tamara replied.

'Are you a journalist?' Paula had won a scholarship to one of the stuffiest formerly men's colleges at Oxford. She was quick on the uptake. Tamara looked thoughtfully at her clever face: thin lips, narrow cheeks, straight, dark brows above straight-aimed, dark eyes. She was an only child. Her mother had founded the Buriton branch of the Society for Gifted Children, writing peevish letters to the local paper about the problems faced by their parents. They attracted slight sympathy, but Tamara, recognising an uncompromising intelligence, felt a little sorry for the girl's less intelligent parent.

Tamara decided to be truthful about facts though not about inferences. Paula, fascinated by what she heard about the events at Qasr Samaan, was only too willing to talk about her friend Polly.

'The trouble with Polly is that she's cleverer than she needs to be but not as clever as she thinks she is.'

Paula and Polly had met at school. It was really Mrs Crosse's fault, all this, Paula explained, and Tamara refrained from asking what wasn't. 'It's all down to my mother. If she hadn't sent me to that silly school . . .'

The two girls were not together at university. Polly was at one of the remaining all-woman colleges, but her family regarded Paula as a suitable friend and the invitations to dinner and garden and country house parties (palace parties, Paula called them) continued. 'It was my bloody mother who made me ask Polly back,' Paula said. 'You can imagine what my real friends thought of her.'

'So whose idea was it that she should borrow your passport and take your place on the excavation?'

'I suppose it was both of ours. I never wanted to go to Egypt anyway. My father picked up something I said about it, months ago, and organised it all as a treat for me. He went to tremendous trouble. He even paid for the air ticket. I couldn't tell him I never really meant it. Poor bloke, he has enough to put up with round here. So I was moaning about it when I saw Polly, you know how one does. She really did want to go. She was simply dying to. So we agreed to swap.'

'And you were left to tell her family? Rather you than me,' Tamara said.

'Good Lord no. Not myself. I was meant to post a letter Polly had left with me. They would have got it once she was safely there. And while she was on the way, they thought she was staying in our cottage in North Devon. She's been there with us before. Her heavies think it's perfectly safe.'

'You mean they simply never noticed she wasn't there with you?'

'That's right. Well, the middle of winter, we wouldn't have gone outside much anyway. They thought we were staying in bed late and eating and watching television. So Polly could get away in disguise without being noticed. There would have been a bit of trouble – I was going to say she'd got me to cover for her while she had a jaunt for a couple of days. She wrote home that she'd pinched my passport and I didn't know anything about it, but they would never have believed that. They always used to say I was a good influence on her. I'd have stopped being persona grata but that's no hardship as far as I'm concerned. Ma would have minded.' Paula's expression showed how little that would distress her.

'And what you actually did was send anonymous letters about kidnaps and ransoms . . .'

'It was brilliant. It really worked. We weren't sure that it would, you can imagine. It was just that there seemed no harm in trying. I said she'd gone for a stroll one morning and just never come back, as simple as that. I pretended to be frightfully upset. You can imagine the fuss. The questions, the police – I should think they suspected me, but there was nothing they could show against me. Anyway by then she was safely incommunicado in the middle of

Lake Nasser. And the starving Sudanese got three whole planes' full.'

'Which were loaded and ready to fly before you began on this,' Tamara suggested. 'Isn't that what was announced?'

'That doesn't mean a thing. Of course they would never have done it if it hadn't been for the pressure,' Paula insisted.

'There had been pressure in Parliament and the Press too. It does rather sound as though your efforts were . . . superfluous,' Tamara said.

'You can think that if you want to,' Paula told her. 'I know what happened.'

A willed blindness, curious facet of someone who seemed otherwise so intelligent. She makes me feel old, Tamara thought. Aloud, she said, 'What I do think is that what you did was rather ruthless, to put it mildly. Not to mention what Polly did. I mean, your families . . .'

'I am ruthless, and proud of it. But the thing about Polly is that she knows what she wants and makes damn sure she gets it. And what she doesn't want. She's spoilt, which is probably inevitable in her circumstances. But it's partly because she is quite smart, in an unintellectual sort of way. You could call her cunning, underneath that deep, invariable, completely artificial surface.'

This girl hates her supposed friend, Tamara thought. This is the resentment of the object of kindness. Polly would think that Paula was biting the hand that fed her with attention and status.

'The thing is,' Paula went on, 'that Polly has never had to learn that some people won't do what she wants.'

'In spite of going to an ordinary school?'

'Ordinary! Snobby and exclusive more like. I told you, if my mother hadn't wanted me to make what she calls suitable friends I'd have gone to the comprehensive like everyone else and never met Polly in the first place.'

'Even if it was snobby, they can't have given Polly special treatment,' Tamara said.

'Maybe not special, but unnatural. It rang false. And so does she. Somewhere inside her there is a nugget of certainty that she really is different from other people, not made of common clay. Oh, they all disguise it, they know they mustn't let it show, but they have all got it. It's innate.'

'She's capable of anything is she?' Tamara said casually.

'I'd say so, murder included. Did she do it? When you came back two people short from Qasr Samaan . . . ?'

Tamara felt a little sympathy for the mother of the gifted child. She parried questions with difficulty and regretted bringing them upon herself. She had spent too much time with people whose brains were blunter than her own.

'The only solution is for you to recruit Paula Crosse to Department E immediately,' she told Mr Black later. 'She's sharp, ruthless and not overburdened by conscience and qualms.'

'You could be describing yourself,' he said.

23

The inquests on Vanessa Papillon and John Benson took place discreetly and with surprisingly little publicity. The flame of Vanessa's fame had depended on her being there to feed and fan it. She would have been mortified to know how ephemeral it was.

John Benson's body was never found. Vanessa's had been reburied in the Protestant cemetery in Aswan, beside the European consumptives of the last century whose quest for health had failed. Giles Needham had been represented by the expedition's doctor, who told the one agency reporter present that the archaeologists could not leave their work, already behind schedule as it was. The season was due to end in May. Vanessa's employers sent a news agency's Middle East correspondent to represent them, and paid for a headstone on which only her assumed name was carved.

The coroner heard evidence that the two people had died, and reached verdicts as to how: accidental death from food poisoning in one case, misadventure, resulting in drowning in the other. Sympathy was extended to Vanessa's family, which consisted of two second cousins, and to Ann Benson.

There was not much publicity. It was old news, and only those determined not to revive it knew that it would be worth doing so. The hearings had been carefully arranged to be in an obscure place; Vera Pritchard was an obscure name; and the coroner had been guided to say that evidence from two witnesses would be enough. The girl whose name appeared in the evidence as Paula Crosse did not attend.

Nor did she appear at other public functions, or agree to see anyone who might ask awkward questions in private.

Tamara's requests for an audience were stalled, queried and leisurely refused. By the time that it was clear Polly would not see her in Scotland, a smart operator with a camera had shown the world that Polly was back in London.

There she was even more impregnable. The barriers of courtesy and courtliness were like velvet padded cast-iron. So long as Polly stayed behind them she remained inaccessible.

She was not to return to college. The announcement said she might be at risk there, and few who read it knew that she was threatened more by wilfulness than abduction.

There followed a renewed flurry of complaints that no arrests had been made. If Scotland Yard was baffled, it shouldn't be. Kidnapping a princess, even a minor one, was not any common or garden crime, which it might be forgivable to leave unsolved. Royal lives are more precious – why else would they be more protected? The police claimed to be following up leads, but there was no evidence of decisive action. It simply was not good enough.

Meanwhile, but for that one snap of Polly being driven in through gates that closed rapidly behind her, there had been no sighting either by Tamara or by the many media hunters who were after the same quarry.

The protectors of Polly's family and its dignity had closed ranks around her. Seeming, not being, was what mattered to them. They did not care what she might have done so long as nobody said she had done it.

A serious police officer, a senior civil servant, and an utterly superior royal one had listened to Tamara's suspicions. If it had not been for Tom Black what she suggested would have been dismissed with respective incredulity, indifference and outrage. Even in his validating presence, only the policeman was prepared to consider the story interesting. The civil servant said it would be better forgotten. The royal servant promised retribution for anyone who remembered it.

'There go your chances of any honours,' Tom Black told Tamara. He was a Commander of the British Empire himself, a misleading title which came with a civil servant's rations, he always said. He had earned others, but kept quiet about them. The DSO, the Legion d'Honneur and the other decorations which at various stages in his varied career he had earned were too showy for a man whose life depended on anonymity.

Tamara was entitled to an alphabet of academic distinctions and did not care if she never added to it.

'You did say yourself that you weren't paid to be a detective,' Tom Black reminded her.

And nor she was; but Tamara could not on that account suppress her curiosity even though her thoughts were as sterile and unproductive as they had been since the day she arrived back in England in March.

She went over and over the facts and her suspicions. It was impossible to think herself back to Qasr Samaan. That hot, remote, obsessive place had completely filled her mind while she was there, as though nowhere else existed. In London, on slimy pavements under dripping plane trees it seemed an illusion.

Tamara was stuck with her book. Working as a freelance to her own timetable was less restful than she expected when she gave up her job. For reassurance she went to stay with Thea Crawford who said she had heard Giles Needham lecturing to the Egypt Exploration Society. He had, as Thea put it, run a mile at the sight of her.

It was the end of term. Paula Crosse had taken her first-class degree and been offered a job with the World Bank.

An advertisement appeared in the *Spectator*, offering country-house weekends at Fernley, with cordon bleu cookery by Ann Benson and English literature and poetry seminars conducted by Timothy Knipe. Mr Black forwarded a cutting from the *Cambridge Evening News* in which Dame Betty Macmillan advertised for a tenant for her basement flat in Newnham village. The literary gossip was of a major work by Max Solomon, due out in September and certain to win every prize going. Blooms Holdings, the parent company through which Hugo Bloom had conducted his multifarious businesses, was taken over at great profit to its shareholders by a recently denationalised company in which the government held 49% of the shares.

In August an unexpected, unpredicted, entirely surprising announcement was made by the royal press officer. Princess Mary was engaged to marry Giles William Fairfax Needham.

24

All but one of the people who had observed Polly and Giles at Qasr Samaan were invited to their wedding. All but two gave interviews and told variously truthful or edited details of the events there.

Janet Macmillan's mother refused the invitation on her daughter's behalf, and forwarded it to her for information. Janet had gone to America to work on the new epilepsy treatment. The industrial security ensured by her new employer was rigid. Nobody could find her to ask questions about Qasr Samaan and Polly.

Of the others, some dined out on the story, some raked the money in. Those who had recognised Polly did not admit it. Ann Benson and Timothy Knipe, who hadn't, said they had known all along.

Jonty Solomon wrote a hasty synopsis for a book in which he would tell the inside story of Qasr Samaan, received a lot of money in advance of the rest of the manuscript, and was offered his own chat show. His father said nothing but smiled benignly.

Public opinion was that Polly's escapade was romantic, forgivable and justified by events. The starving Sudanese had been fed – admittedly the government claimed that they would have been fed, and had been going to be fed, without the irrelevance of two girls' adolescent caper – and a princess had found true love. Some policemen had wasted their time but only two daily newspapers and one weekly allowed their columnists to complain of that. Paula Crosse's offer of a job with the World Bank was withdrawn, but she was immediately invited to join an international organisation for famine relief instead. Princess Mary became its British patron.

Ann Benson rang Tamara a week before the wedding. 'We must have a get together. Isn't it wonderful? Of course I knew it all along.'

'What did you know?'

'Who Polly was, of course. I've always been observant about people. Of course poor John didn't notice anything and nor did dear Hugo. I don't know what's happened to him, by the way, there has been no word from him since I got back from Egypt and no answer to his telephone either. I would have thought that the least he could do would be to come and see me. But I suppose they'll have to ask him to Polly's wedding too. I'd better not call her that; it might slip out when I see her. Do you think "sir" would be correct for Giles now? And what about a present? I wanted to ask your advice – shall I send them one of John's little Egyptian treasures that I brought back? I gave one or two to Timothy's children. They come here every weekend. I want them to come and live here; Fernley has so much to offer the young. Inigo says he's going to be an archaeologist like Mr Needham when he's grown-up. Do you think they would like that little alabaster dish? Timothy says it isn't necessary but after we spent all that time together I feel we are almost family. Do you think we'll all sit together in the church? I am having an outfit made. It's so important. The cameras will be on us. John would not have been able to bear it.'

In recent years royal weddings had been regularly supplied as an equivalent of Roman circuses, to distract the restless populace, Tamara said. Ann Benson, who thought it was very nice to read good news for a change instead of bad, did not understand what Tamara was talking about. Timothy

Knipe disapproved of the way so many people made money out of them.

Giles submitted to being groomed and paraded with a meekness that made Tamara suspect a more powerful motive than love.

It was announced that Britton's Best, the supermarket chain, had agreed to fund all future seasons at Qasr Samaan. A cigarette manufacturer was to sponsor an exhibition, and a series of lectures given by Giles would be named after a popular brand of cat food.

He would have no future problems in laying on excavations and research projects. Donors of money and equipment would be queueing up to hand them over. To pass every non-digging season with Polly and make a few public appearances were a small price to pay for a secure future of discovering the past.

Two days before the wedding Hugo Bloom was released. The Israelis swapped him for a pair of young Egyptians accused of plotting sabotage.

Hugo knew better than to return to Britain. He might not be charged with any offence; there might not be any illegality he could be charged with. But he was not going to risk it. His information for Tamara Hoyland must be told outside the jurisdiction or not at all. He had to go to New York and was willing to stopover in Dublin. To no further effort and no closer meeting place would he go.

The ambivalence of the Irish to the British monarchy was much in evidence in the Dublin hotel. Photographs of the happy couple were displayed everywhere, along with informative family trees that explained Polly's relatively obscure significance in genealogical terms. Above or beside, was the tricolour; and some slogan-printed stickers cursed the ancient enemy.

An extra television screen had been set up in the hotel lounge. It was tuned to London. Dress-guesses and jollity interrupted shots of the processional route, the bunting and the crowds.

Hugo was late. Due in time for dinner, he had not turned up for breakfast. His aeroplane's estimated time of arrival was deferred further with each telephone call Tamara made to enquire about it.

She should have caught a flight to London at dawn.

'You'll get a better view on television,' Tom Black said. He thought it was important to hear Hugo Bloom's testimony. 'It may be the only chance, while he's just freed and feeling free.'

'All the same, I would have liked to be there.' Tamara's new Jean Muir dress was waiting in her cupboard at home. She had bought a magnificent hat. She had been looking forward to concentrating on straightforward vanities.

'Never mind,' Mr Black shouted down the bad line. 'Knowledge is power.'

Tamara never drank during the day. Alcohol now would curdle the breakfast coffee. On the screen champagne corks were popping as fashion forecasters described what the wedding guests ought to wear.

'Whisky sour,' Tamara told the barman gloomily.

'Drinking their health?'

'No, drowning my sorrows,' she said, and they were on their last gasp when Hugo Bloom joined her.

Tamara stared at him over the rim of her glass. Thinner, paler, with white hair at the temples, he looked distinguished still, but not martial.

'I am afraid I am too late,' he said.

'Engine trouble?'

'Weeks late, I meant. There was a delay in arranging the exchange. The Israelis had nobody suitable to offer.'

'Someone was found in the end?'

'A pair of nice young ornithologists, doing no harm to anyone in the Negev. But they had to be kept in prison for a little while to make it seem convincing. I should have been here sooner otherwise.'

'You must be valuable.'

'Not especially. One coup years ago when I recognised a face in the safe house's garden; and then an aeon of pretending to love the clarinet and going out for afternoon walks. The few titbits I garnered never seemed worth the effort. Nothing was nearly as useful as Janet's data would have been. But all we can do is our best, the likes of you and me.'

'And suffer for it,' Tamara said. It was the risk they took, the likes of Tamara and Hugo. She felt a closer kinship with him, suddenly, than with any man since her friend Ian Barnes, a spy himself, had been killed. That acceptance of danger changed people. It was pointless to imagine that a man who knew nothing of it could know anything of her. 'At least they got you out in the end.'

'We believe in paying our debts.'

'We?'

'I am an Israeli now. But I owe you a lot.'

'Me?'

'Your country.'

'Yours too, surely.'

'I was born here in Dublin. My family were Jews. I grew up in Belfast and grew rich in London. But that's over. This is by way of a leaving present. Call it a bread-and-butter letter, so long delayed, I fear, as to be worse than none. My news will not be welcome.'

Since Polly's wedding was of more social than dynastic or constitutional significance, there was to be none of the input (in the television commentator's words) from the armed services that had decorated previous, more important royal weddings. But her father had served in a regiment whose dress uniform was impractically glamorous, and a guard of honour lined the way from carriage to church at least, if not the route, which was, instead, marked by rows of London policemen, facing the spectators rather than the spectacle.

The processions of guests had begun. Sounds of approval surged cheerily into the small bar. A group of Americans ordered champagne cocktails.

'That sounds a good idea,' Tamara said.

Hugo ordered Bollinger. 'But I am afraid you aren't going to feel like celebrating.'

'I suppose you actually saw Polly,' Tamara said.

'Polly? No, I heard Giles.'

If he had been certain of his guess about Tamara's role, Hugo would have said something at the time, even though he too was primarily interested in Janet.

He had picked up the hint of her scientific discovery quite by accident, at a dinner party given by one of his customers. It seemed a good idea to follow her to Egypt, partly for commercial reasons – there might have been a big profit in it for him – but especially for patriotic ones.

'As an Israeli?' Tamara asked.

'Or an Irishman. They have a lot in common, including short, perilous frontiers.'

To Hugo, as he tried to win Janet's confidence and confidences, what the others at Qasr Samaan got up to was irrelevant.

Tamara very badly wanted not to hear what Giles Needham had got up to.

He was leaving Claridges, where he had spent the previous night.

'Good-looking bugger, you have to give him that,' Hugo said judiciously. Giles had achieved an impassivity of feature that would serve him well in his new life. He walked across the pavement to the waiting cars like a batsman to his wicket. The tails of his morning coat flapped in the wet wind.

The cameras zoomed onto his unsmiling mouth, onto the unfocused eyes that were not drawn to any of the shouting watchers.

'Butchering Giles to make a Roman holiday?' Tamara said.

'They still have the death penalty for murder in Egypt,' Hugo replied.

The bride was starting her short journey. Inside her glass show case Polly sat beaming and waving. 'A beautiful bride,' the voices were saying in the hotel bar and out on the air. 'What a lovely bride.' An instant jabber of analysis began about her dress and veil. Tiaras and lace, buttons and bows fluttered along the sound waves.

'I heard them,' Hugo said. 'I don't know whether anything could have been done to stop this if I had been able to let you know before. I was on my usual morning jog, a shorter route, though, because I had started late. All this happened just round the corner from the camp. John Benson had followed Giles out. He cornered him to ask for authentications of a whole lot of fake antiquities. Giles refused, Benson said he would tell the world about Polly, and Giles knocked him out. I heard the connection, and then the splash.'

'But you did nothing about it?'

'What should I have done? But in fact, I didn't realise quite what I had heard. It was only later that the sound that preceded the splash explained itself in my memory. At the time I thought Benson was having a well-deserved ducking.'

Polly had reached the church, to a roar of welcome and encouragement. 'Good luck, girl,' her well wishers shouted.

'It's bad luck on Polly,' Tamara said remorsefully.

'She was there at the time too.'

Polly must have seen the whole thing. Hugo thought that she and Giles had gone out together that morning. She could have saved John Benson at least, even if she could not stop Giles hitting him.

'How do you know it wasn't Polly who hit him then?'

'That little creature?'

Polly was three inches taller than Tamara. Her tiara was at about the level of her father's eyes as they walked slowly up the long aisle, but it did not reach Giles's shoulder. Giles did not turn to greet her, but waited, face forward, like an ox in a slaughter-house. Only the archbishop's mitre equalled his height.

'That can't all be make-up,' Hugo said. 'You would hardly think that it was the same girl. Remember what she looked like when we first saw her?'

'All girls look good at their own weddings.'

'Perhaps the stuff Vanessa gave her did the trick?'

'What stuff?'

'Some potion for her complexion. It was when Vanessa was talking about their return to England, and what she'd be saying about Polly's escapade. You know what a cat she was. She said Polly wouldn't want to appear with all those spots, and what about trying this stuff she imported from Indonesia. Poisonous but effective, she said, don't drink it by mistake.'

'I think I had better have another drink,' Tamara said. Gloomily she listened to the familiar words.

The archbishop whispered his homily to the happy couple. Meanwhile the camera's eye swooped around the congregation. In the bar, heavy drinkers giggled at the guests' clothes.

Tamara was tipsy, an unusual state for her; but this was an unusual day. A marriage was taking place between two people who knew the worst about each other; and about whom not much worse could be known.

But mutual connivance or even mutual blackmail might be as good a starting point for marriage as any other reciprocated emotion. It might fasten a tighter bond.

Gold foil and corks were heaped up behind the bar. A quick picture on the screen of the crowds ready to greet the happy couple showed that inhibitions had been relaxed there too.

Tamara lifted her glass of golden bubbles. 'To a well matched pair,' she said.

The archbishop had pronounced them man and wife. In a moment Giles and Polly would walk out of the church and into life together. For what Polly wanted, Polly always got.